The Freedom Artist

BEN OKRI won the Booker prize in 1991 for *The Famished Road*. He has published ten novels, four volumes of short stories, four books of essays, and four collections of poems. His work has been translated into more than twenty-six languages. He also writes plays and filmscripts. He is a Fellow of the Royal Society of Literature, a vice-president of English PEN and has been awarded the OBE as well as numerous international prizes and honorary doctorates. Born in Nigeria, he lives in London.

ALSO BY BEN OKRI

FICTION

Flowers and Shadows
The Landscapes Within
Incidents at the Shrine
Stars of the New Curfew
The Famished Road
Songs of Enchantment
Astonishing the Gods
Dangerous Love
Infinite Riches
In Arcadia
Starbook
The Comic Destiny
(previously *Tales of Freedom*)
The Age of Magic
The Magic Lamp

ESSAYS

Birds of Heaven
A Way of Being Free
The Mystery Feast
A Time for New Dreams

POETRY

An African Elegy
Mental Fight
Wild
Rise Like Lions (Anthology)

PLAYS

The Outsider

The
Freedom
Artist

BEN OKRI

HEAD
of ZEUS

First published in the UK in 2019 by Head of Zeus Ltd

9 7 5 3 1 2 4 6 8

A catalogue record for this book is available from
the British Library.

ISBN (HB): 9781788549592
ISBN (XTPB): 9781788549608
ISBN (E): 9781788549585

Typeset by Adrian McLaughlin

Printed and bound in Great Britain by
CPI Group (UK) Ltd, Croydon CR0 4YY

Head of Zeus Ltd
First Floor East
5–8 Hardwick Street
London EC1R 4RG

WWW.HEADOFZEUS.COM

To Charlotte Jarvis
For the along

Acknowledgments

I wish to say a special thanks to the following people: to my editor, Maggie McKernan; to my agent, Georgina Capel; to R.C; to the inimitable Anthony Cheetham; and to all the good people at Head of Zeus.

Read slowly

Everything sacred, that intends to remain so, must cover itself in mystery.

SENGHOR

OVERTURE

1

It is written in the oldest legends that all are born in prison. This prison is all they know. Literature describes life in it. Religion hints at redemption from it. Having lived here all their lives, humans have ceased to see it as a prison.

'This is all there is,' the realists said, 'so we might as well make the most of it.'

That had been the dominant thought for thousands of years. Under its influence humans had created civilisations all over the world. They had waged wars, erected pyramids and punctuated the silent text of the earth with temples.

To create a reality more real than the world was their idea of perfection. Music filled the lands with the sistrum and the lyre, the flute and the drum. They created music of such beauty that they temporarily forgot their underlying misery. Their civilisations became so successful that they forgot they were in prison. They began to think they were free.

2

Through the years of living and dying people forgot they were in prison. But they could not reconcile the splendour of their condition with the underlying misery of their lives, as they emerged on earth and retreated into dust. They felt the misery even in the splendour.

From time to time they heard rumours, whispered by poets and uttered by the mad, that they were all prisoners. They were born that way and would die that way. These rumours bothered the people.

Every now and then a philosopher, poring over the ancient legends, would come upon a fragment of the founding myth. One such philosopher, sharing his discovery, wrote:

'Humans are born in prison, and everywhere think they are free.'

This caused shock-waves across the world. It became necessary for the authorities to proscribe these ideas or to distort them.

They need not have bothered. People do not believe that which does not please them. They preferred new myths which celebrated their freedom.

This state of affairs continued for a long time. There were wars, famines, floods, economic disasters and all the vicissitudes which attend the human estate.

Things might have gone on in the same way were it not for an event which disturbed their age-old certainties.

3

One day a man stared at the reflection of the sun in a lake. Lost in reverie, he found himself somewhere he had never been before. It was nothing like the earth. When he came back to himself he was still sitting by the lake. He told some friends about this experience, but they regarded it as a lapse of the mind.

On a splendid moonlit night a young girl was reading one of the old myths. While she read she found herself on the bank of a river of light. It was like nowhere on earth. Its beauty startled her back to the room where she had been reading. She told the experience to her parents and they said she must have been daydreaming.

These anomalies were never reported to the authorities. They never appeared in the rumour sections of the newspapers. But they began the age of disquiet.

Not long afterwards, on a cold and silent night, a cry was heard. Someone had escaped the prison of the world. The cry announced the extraordinary life beyond. This was not a cry of lamentation, but of exultation. It was heard on the edge of the desert. It was heard once and never again. That one cry was enough to infect the world with unease.

4

There are few things as haunting as a question posed in the night. For the first time in centuries the notion that the world was a prison was heard again. The founding myth, long forgotten, was beginning to speak.

New versions of the founding myth had been gaining mysterious circulation. In some versions it wasn't the earth that was the prison, it was the universe. For many this was an intolerable notion. Some thought it funny that people who accepted the limits of the earth could not accept the confinement of the universe. Which was better, they asked: to be free on earth or a prisoner in the universe?

Then a radical version of the founding myth appeared. It was not the earth or the universe that was the prison, it was the body.

This was one prison too many and riots broke out everywhere. The authorities tried to suppress these subversive ideas. The police confiscated large numbers of books. They imprisoned publishers and booksellers. They destroyed all forms of printing. These versions of the founding myth were burnt in public squares. People were forbidden to read them, under punishment of death.

5

But it was too late. The damage had been done. The idea had entered the bloodstream of the world. A few people, who were terminally ill anyway, took their lives because they wanted to escape the prison of their bodies. The idea made life for them not worth living.

Questions began to roam the world. If you are a prisoner in your body, how can you find freedom? Who put you in the prison of your body? If you are in the prison of your body, who is the prisoner?

The last question caused the greatest perplexity of all. One night the question appeared on the walls of buildings. It flowered on the streets, was painted on cars and billboards, stencilled on walls, spray-painted on buses. The question was everywhere.

WHO IS THE PRISONER?

At this point, the authorities decided to act. Things had gone too far. The questions had begun to induce lethargy, despair, rebellion and riots in the populace. The perpetrators of these intolerable questions had to be found and destroyed so that society might recover its equilibrium. Spies and informers infiltrated the populace to root out those responsible for what was becoming known as the age of anxiety.

6

It is written, in a lesser legend, that in a prison the size of a country there were prisoners who had been there for generations. Their original crimes had been forgotten in the fog of time. Families gave rise to families and were scattered through the length and breadth of the vast prison. There were whole tribes of eternal prisoners.

At first the prison was modest. Then the accumulation of acts designated as crimes led to an astronomical multiplication of prisoners. Anything could be a crime: deviation from normal thought, unusualness in dress, questions about the nature of time, speculations about the nature of the soul, paintings that distort reality, writings that cause unease, the inclination to think too much. The most serious crimes were those that questioned the nature of reality.

At some time or other most people found themselves on the wrong side of the law. It became necessary to extend the prison till it took on the proportions of a country. Then it was proposed that an entire continent be devoted to containing the exploding criminal population that was humanity. Soon there were more people in prison than outside it.

The prison became the world.

7

Meanwhile there were catastrophes across the earth. Sea levels had risen. Forests had become sparse. Trees and flowers were perishing everywhere. Tropical countries had become cold, and the cold countries had become hot.

The rich had taken over the earth. They lived in heavily fortified houses while the poor fought for food, marauded the streets, and slept in the open.

Books had become rare. All knowledge existed in immaterial form. Centuries of being attached to the machine had atrophied the languages of the earth. Slowly the races returned to a primitive form of speech. Ideas were communicated in grunts. Shrugs and facial expressions were the new vocabulary.

The few that retained the power of language kept to themselves. Lest their ability drew scorn upon them, they didn't speak in public. The economy was managed by a handful of super-bankers. Newspapers ceased to exist. Except as organs of the state. Television was run by the people. Programmes consisted of the daily life of the populace. Radio stations had fallen to ranters. Day-long harangues dominated the airwaves.

Anomie had spread across the world.

BOOK ONE

1

In a yellow house an old man was being read to by a boy. They took turns reading to one another, and now it was the boy's turn. The boy's name was Mirababa. He was reading the tale of the child who climbed a ladder that led to another world where he was given magic gifts by giants.

He stopped reading for a moment.

'Is it true,' he said, 'that there is another world beyond ours?'

The old man was silent for a long time. Mirababa was used to these silences and had learnt to read them. From the old man's silence this is what the boy read: 'It was asking questions that got our ancestors into this place. Yet you go on asking them?'

This is what the boy sensed all his life whenever he asked a question that was not answered. He came to understand that questions were not answered by answers. They were answered by subtleties of silence.

Mirababa was about to go on reading when to his surprise the old man began to speak. He spoke in a rasping, but soothing voice. It may have been approaching death that moved the old man to such an uncharacteristic act.

'One day, my boy, you must take a leap into the unknown and discover what has been hidden from us…'

The old man paused. Mirababa heard, in the silence that followed, the beating of an eagle's wing outside the window.

For a moment he heard his own heartbeat. The old man had not answered his question, but had only caused him to listen more intently to the silence.

Mirababa absorbed the silence for a while and then began reading again. He had read no more than a few words when the old man interrupted him.

'The only way to go beyond is to go in.'

'Go in?'

'Where did the child go, in the story you've been reading to me?'

'He climbed up a ladder to another world.'

'Where did he go?'

'Up.'

'Up is in.'

The old man paused.

'Do you remember the tale I read to you about the hero who was trying to get back home?'

'The one where he blinded a one-eyed giant and listened to the siren's songs?'

'That one. Where was he going?'

'Home.'

'Going home is going in.'

'In to where?'

The old man paused. This time he shut his eyes as if weary. The boy began listening to the silence, but the old man said:

'Don't be like the rest of us. Follow your nature. Follow your questions. Those who try to escape prison end up in another one. Escape that one and they find themselves in another. This world is a succession of prisons and there is no escaping the prison of the world. In our family we have broken out of the prison beyond prison and the prisons beyond that. I'm the last in the line.'

The old man paused, eyes still shut. His voice was lower when he began speaking again.

'I know that the solution is not out there. For there are only prisons followed by prisons, to the horizon of all things. Astronauts who have been to outer space have not been able to escape the prison of the universe. We have tried every way, except one.'

'Which one is that, Grandad?'

'I am an old man listening to what the eagle's wing says.'

'What does the eagle's wing say?'

'It says it's time to go home.'

'But you are home.'

'I'm an old man who has spent his life in prison and dreams only of freedom.'

'What is freedom, Grandad?'

'I dream of the source of the sea. Your voice reminds me of home.' The old man's voice was growing fainter. 'I won't live to see the face of the full moon. Listen to me. This is what was handed down to me by the heroes of old. Everything we need to know is concealed in what we most take for granted. Everyone has sought this elixir called freedom. They have sought it for thousands of years. There have been rumours that one unique person found it and passed on the secret in clues hidden in the ancient myths. Apparently two or three other people have found it too, but we don't know for sure. No one has found it from the ancient times till now.'

The old man allowed a longer silence to infiltrate his words.

'I have travelled all the routes on the map. I have exhausted the old road. My way has failed, and we are still here, in prison. Now it's your turn. It's your time. Find the elixir of freedom, and bring it back to the people, that we may all be free. If not, we will perish. We will perish of hopelessness.'

The old man stopped. He opened his eyes, and was about to resume, when he found that the boy had fallen asleep.

2

In another house, early in the evening, Amalantis was listening to her lover with a listless air.

His name was Karnak. He was a fine young man with gentle features and doe-like eyes. He was at an in-between stage in his life, awaiting employment. He was speaking of the charm of her cheeks, the bewitchment of her eyes, and the firm grace of her body. He was passionately in love with her. But for some time now she had been feeling a strange emptiness. The more people praised her beauty, the emptier she felt.

It had begun one morning long ago when she was staring into a mirror. As she gazed at her face someone in the mirror appeared to wink at her. She became aware that there was someone inside her who wasn't her. The more she looked the more she felt that someone other than her was trapped behind her face. Who is behind that mask that everyone thinks is me, she wondered. This question was the beginning of her troubles.

She got it into her head that whoever was behind her face was a prisoner. She felt imprisoned within herself. It was a notion that brought panic. She could not share this notion with anyone.

Everybody thought Amalantis beautiful. But the more people praised her beauty, the more she felt like a fraud.

This made her silent in the face of adulation, deepening her mystery, increasing the adulation. Often lost in thought, she felt estranged from the truth of life, and began to brood. That was long ago.

When Karnak poured praises on her, she could think of nothing to say except what she should not say.

'Your praise makes me ill.'

'I'm sorry to hear that.'

'Why don't we talk about something more intriguing?'

'Like what?'

'Like… who do you think the prisoner is?'

Karnak was startled, as if stung by a snake.

'Prisoner? What prisoner?'

'You know, the graffiti they keep trying to get rid of? The stuff that keeps appearing everywhere?'

'What're you talking about?'

'Who is the prisoner?'

Karnak shut the door quickly.

'We're not supposed to say that word. It could get us into trouble. We could be put away for it.'

'Are you afraid of the truth too?'

'Truth? What truth?'

'You know everyone's asking the question.'

'But they're not asking it out loud. Don't say that word again. Don't say anything.'

Amalantis didn't speak for a while but stared thoughtfully out of the window.

'I would like to know,' she said eventually, 'who the prisoner is.'

'Why?'

At that moment, they heard three knocks at the door. The young lover opened the door and saw three men standing there. They were dressed identically in grey suits and ties. They went over to the girl and marched her out to the road, where a grey van was already waiting.

Amalantis was silent as she was led away. Karnak found himself in the doorway, watching as if in a dream. She was hoisted into the back of the van. Then it pulled away. Not one of the men had spoken a single word.

3

There were many such arrests throughout the land. They took place at all hours of the day or night. People were arrested while they slept, in the middle of their dreams, or while they were at work. Nobody protested. Those who came to do the arresting did not speak. Their presence was enough. Those arrested were taken to unknown places, never heard from again.

A strange silence spread across the land. The streets gradually emptied. Those who were not arrested, but witnessed the arrests of others, went around in a constant state of fear. People spoke less and less to each other. Their conversation became neutral. They stopped looking one another in the eye. No laughter was heard in the streets. A gloomy mood pervaded the land.

Naturally, the quality of language changed. Certain words became suspicious and vanished from public life. Words like 'hope', 'rights', 'truth'. Anyone heard uttering those words found empty spaces around them. It wasn't long before anyone using the word 'freedom' was suspected of harbouring dangerous intentions.

The question which appeared on walls did not go away just because the authorities grew more ruthless. If anything the question and its appearance in public spaces grew more audacious.

On a bright morning the wind would blow square bits of paper among the populace. On these miniature bills was the question: WHO IS THE PRISONER?

Silence had only multiplied the power of the question.

4

There were, in those times, two classes of people. One, the overwhelming majority, were the 'normal' people. They did not speak much. They did their work, fulfilled their obligations, raised their families, read the newspapers, absorbed all they read, watched television, and believed all they saw. They kept their nightmares to themselves. They constituted the highest presence in hospital wards and psychiatric clinics. They had, as a running music in their heads, a steady, unchanging drone.

And yet, at night, in room after room, across council estates or in rich suburbs, screams could be heard coming from their beds. They shouted in their sleep and howled like frightened animals. This could be heard at night all across the land. It became so common that soon it was considered the normal mode of sleep. That is to say no one noticed it any more.

5

The second kind of people looked like the first except for one thing. They were more alert. They didn't sleep much at night. Their eyes had a constant wakefulness. They didn't read the newspapers, treated television as a daily farce, and believed nothing of what they saw or heard. They were the few.

They drank water, stared at the sky, listened to the wind, and paid attention to everything. They were generally silent. If addressed or asked a question they shrugged. They spoke gently. They smiled mysteriously, incompletely, an inward smile made almost visible.

They worked as little as possible and yet were immensely productive. They seemed solitary, but were not lonely. They could often be heard humming a piece of music to themselves. They ventured no philosophy, and offered no resistance. They seemed absent when present. But they were present when absent.

They did not scream in their sleep and never had nightmares. They were unnoticeable, indistinguishable. But a strange light hovered in the space they had vacated. They were deep breathers and had a curious quality of agelessness about their features.

They did not hear an unchanging background drone in their heads. They heard a pure silence, the mildest fragrance of a melody.

More than anything else it was her beauty that frightened him.

'How can you be so beautiful and still be human?' he asked.

'Am I beautiful?'

'You know you are.'

'Let me show you what beauty is,' she said.

Then she got him to take a long walk with her. It was early in the evening. She took him to the far fields on the edge of the city. Gentle howls were drifting across from the trees.

'Wait here,' she said.

They stood for ten minutes and nothing happened. Then just as he was beginning to feel restless he saw these horses in the field. He didn't know where they came from. They just seemed to appear. They were huge and their bodies slick and fine. There were black horses and white ones and horses that were almost golden in colour. They grazed and played and galloped, their manes blowing in the light wind.

'That's beautiful,' she said, after they stared at the horses a long time in silence.

On the way back they passed an old woman in a doorway. She sat in the doorway, looking unhappy and a little lost.

'That's beautiful too,' Amalantis said.

'That old woman who looked sad?'

'Yes,' she said. 'That's one of the most beautiful people I know.'

Karnak looked back at the old lady, who was weeping now. Amalantis said:

24

'You go on home. I have to help her.'

'But you don't even know her.'

'I do now,' she said, and went back to the old lady.

Karnak watched her talking to the old lady for a long time. He waited in the shadow of the building. Then after a while the old lady and Amalantis went into the house. Karnak sat and leant against the wall and waited. He fell asleep. When he woke up he found Amalantis sitting next to him, watching him with a tender expression in her eyes.

'Why didn't you wake me?'

'Thank you for waiting for me,' she said.

'Why didn't you wake me, though?'

'Because I kept thinking how beautiful you looked. I wanted to show you what beauty was and didn't quite know how.'

'What happened with the old woman?'

'She just wants to die.'

'But why?' Karnak asked, looking at her.

Amalantis didn't reply. She merely looked at him as if he should know the answer already.

He didn't then, and it bewildered him.

6

The old man was found dead on the night of the full moon, sitting upright in his chair, with an open book in his lap. His face was at peace. Those who looked closely saw a faint smile on his lips.

He had bequeathed his earthly possessions to his family, urging them to keep alive the old myths now being forgotten. To the boy, with whom he spent the last months reading, he bequeathed a particular manuscript. It was to be read only by him, when he was ready.

The manuscript was written in the old hand, which few people could read. It was called *The Legend of the Prison*.

7

The boy did not weep at the old man's funeral. Nor did any-one else. He was one of the secret heroes of the land. His death was an occasion for celebration, silence, and poetry. The old bards appeared among them. As the body was being transmuted into the golden ash of his final estate, they recited the ancient myths in deep intonations. With music wrung from the lyre and the drum, their voices accompanied the flight of the old man's soul to Elysium.

At the appointed time, the old bards came for Mirababa and led him into the forest. This was in accordance with the ancient custom which dictated that with the death of an old myth-maker a new one is initiated. The old man's death was the beginning of the boy's life.

That night many in the land noticed the flight of a white eagle. It seemed to fly straight into the unnatural whiteness of the full moon.

8

Karnak had watched helplessly from the door while that flower of the land was taken away. Like a sacrificial lamb, she had gone without a sound of protest. At the door of the van she had turned her head to look back at him. A mysterious smile trembled on her lips. With an inexplicable movement of her head, a lifting of her face, she got into the back of the van and was driven away.

The young lover was rooted to the spot, as if under a spell. He stared at the empty space where he had last seen the strange smile on her face. He stared and saw nothing. He thought nothing.

A numbness spread through him. He simply stared. He did not notice the birds whirling in the air. He did not notice passers-by staring at him. Neighbours went past him, said 'hello', and he did not hear them. They noticed his vacancy.

He stood there for a long time. He didn't see the light change in the sky. He didn't see the darkness extending its dominion over the earth. He didn't hear the sounds of the world altered by the vanishing light.

Then a shout in the street woke him from his stupor. When he looked around he saw, to his amazement, that it was already dark. Feeling stiff from standing too long in one place, he shut the door behind him and set off on the long solitary walk to his home through the darkening streets.

As he walked he heard shouts and howls rising from the houses he passed. He heard them one by one, then in twos, then in confused choruses. Then the cries would fall silent. Then suddenly again they would shatter the silence and he would listen to the howls and screams rising from the many houses, from lonely rooms, from crowded bedrooms.

He was never normally out so late, because of the curfew. He was hearing these shouts and cries for the first time. As he listened to them with fear in his heart he wondered what horror was befalling people while they slept.

The howls were loud and frightening. They broke out in sudden wild crescendos or stretched out in long lonely howls and lamentations. Sometimes there would be an extended tiny female whimper. After a while he began to hurry. He could bear the sounds no longer. He muffled his ears with his hands and still he could hear the cries.

Soon he was half-running in the dark. At the crossroads, howls and screams flew at him from several directions. Disorientated, he took a wrong turning and found himself in a common field. The moon shone gently on the trees. The spaces between the trees had a wonderland quality.

The cries became more distant. He rested against a tree and tried to think. He could not think. It occurred to him to begin moving again, to find his way home.

Then he saw figures in the moonlit field, running between the trees. They moved at surprising speed. Before he knew it, they were gone. They went in the direction of the streets, towards the screams, and he decided to follow.

But as he followed them he became aware of a tender fragrance. It was the fragrance of roses.

9

Beyond the common field, at the crossroads where he had taken the wrong turning, he saw one of the figures climbing a fence. He saw another make its way up a billboard. Then there was a third crouching and doing something odd on the street. Then they vanished.

He ran down several streets, searching in the dark for them, barely noticing the cascade of screams pouring out from basements, tower blocks and mansions. He couldn't find them anywhere. It was as though they had melted into the moonlight. Back at the crossroads, on the bare wall of a building, was the painted legend:

WHO IS THE PRISONER?

He panicked at seeing the words he was not even allowed to think. It occurred to him that if he was caught at that moment it might be assumed that he had something to do with the words. Without another thought he began to hurry away from the sight. But as he ran along he saw the question everywhere, freshly painted in red and white. He looked down and saw that he was walking on the question that had been stencilled on the road beneath his feet. It crossed his mind that if the paint was fresh then he would have some of this incriminating paint on the soles of his feet.

He heard whistles and feared that the police were converging on the scene. Fear gave him intelligence. He ran like a rabbit in the first direction that came into his head. He ran back towards the moonlit field.

10

The bards had taken Mirababa deep into the forest. It was very dark in there. He heard the forest noises. Cobwebs stretched across his face. He felt their silken trail on his cheeks. It was a dense forest. Majestic trees rose to the obscure sky. They walked past dark tangles of bushes and wild flowers and vines and clumps of trees. Animals fled at the sound of their feet on the fallen leaves.

The old bards had no lanterns and yet they found their way along the track with unerring precision. They were mostly silent, but now and then the oldest bard made an incantation to the god of night. The intoned vowel, for a moment, caused the wind to be still.

The boy followed obediently. He felt they had been walking all night. At last they emerged into a clearing and he caught his breath in astonishment. In the clearing a still lake hovered.

The lake was darkness itself. A breeze blew across its surface, wrinkling the perfect mirror. As if he had woken from a spell, he saw the moon rippling on the face of the water.

Silently the old bards made him sit at the edge of the lake. Then they retreated into the forest, walking backwards, as though their bodies were made of the substance of the dark.

11

Mirababa gazed at the moon in the lake, drawn into its whiteness. After a long while he felt himself becoming the mirror of the moon, merging into its white form.

It seemed an endless night, and he lost all sense of himself. He no longer knew where he was but he was dimly conscious of white light around him. The forest and the lake had vanished. The nocturnal cries of the forest were silent. Not even the moon remained. There was just the pure space, vast and small at the same time, everywhere and nowhere simultaneously.

A smile, spreading from his feet, travelled up his legs to the pit of his belly. It widened in his chest. The smile soon filled his whole being. Then the cry of an owl penetrated his tranquil mood, and he saw the lake again. The moon was gone. He heard a distinct voice say:

'Go in.'

Without thinking, or maybe with swift thought, he discerned what he must do. With a single agile movement, he dived in.

12

Karnak hid in the field, among the trees. He watched as the police silently invaded the streets, in white vans, in an efficient operation. It was as if they had been lying in wait nearby. Their protective gear gleamed in the dark.

Heavily armed, they patrolled the streets. They went to the backs of houses and to the rooftops. They searched the area thoroughly. When they widened their search to the field where he was hiding, the young lover thought it necessary to flee.

He ran from tree to tree, crouching. He reached a wall, climbed over it and found himself on the back streets. He went on running, still crouching, till he saw a fox near a tree. It regarded him with glimmering eyes. He felt reassured by its presence.

He made his way across the empty road and kept to the shadows. Running and crouching, he came to a neighbourhood he knew. The howls and screams sounded through the closed windows. He listened with a new dread as he made his way home.

In his room he tried not to think about the day. He could not bring himself to face what had happened, what he had witnessed. For the first time in his life, Karnak was confused.

He had been made to believe that the world was the best way it could be. He thought like everyone else. He behaved like everyone else. He had fallen in love the same way everyone else had. He expected his life to be like everyone else's. He expected to get married, to have children, and to scream at night without knowing why.

He never expected that he would have to concern himself with problems. He had accepted that it was forbidden to think or to speak certain words. He accepted it all as the wisdom of the race, the wisdom of the fathers and the mothers.

But he never expected the person he loved most in the world to be taken from him before his very eyes and that he'd be unable to do anything.

He never expected that he would have to ask questions. He didn't know how to ask questions. This was confusing. He had no one to share the feeling with.

Then he began to think about the people he had seen that night running across the field and leaping over the fences. Maybe they could answer some of his questions. Maybe they could help, without getting him into trouble.

13

It was told in a story that one day a boy standing by himself in a garden of sunflowers saw a ladder he had never seen before. Out of curiosity, he climbed the ladder. It grew longer as he climbed. Eventually he found himself in a world where there was no freedom. The people were in chains, but the chains were invisible.

The people were curious about the world the boy had come from. He told them stories about his world and the stories infected people with new ideas. It wasn't long before the authorities heard of the boy from another world who was spreading ideas that caused unrest. The boy was arrested and left in the infinite dungeons, lost and lonely and unmissed.

He might have perished but for the fact that he remembered the magic ladder. After a time in that limbo, he found the ladder, and climbed back down to the world he had come from. But the world he knew had changed in his absence.

When he had climbed the ladder up to that other world, the other world had climbed the ladder down to his. And the other world had infected his with ideas it had never known before, notions of despair, infinite prisons, and a horror of freedom.

The boy learnt too late that to infect a world is also to be infected by that world.

14

Around that time the authorities began prosecuting a ruthless campaign against the question-askers. The brighter minds in the Hierarchy came up with a method of ensuring a spirit of productive obedience. It was the most fiendish and the simplest idea they had had in a long time. They decided to have the old myths altered.

The most prominent scholars in the land, who had been given the highest honours, were commissioned to reinterpret the ancient myths. New versions appeared in the state bookshops and libraries. These were the only bookshops and libraries allowed to exist at that time. The old fairy tales were given new glosses, new clothes. The older versions went out of print. They were no longer relevant. The old myths, in the newest version, were made relevant, brought up to date. Now they anticipated the problems of the day and justified contemporary solutions.

One of the old myths which told the story of a long and difficult homecoming was transformed into a spiritual support for the land in its present time of crisis. Another myth about the voyage of heroes to find a golden pelt came to be about the soldiers of the land finding the golden key to peace, using whatever methods were necessary. The tale about the Emperor's new clothes was rewritten to show the boy praised for noticing how beautiful the Emperor's new clothes were. All tales about people climbing ladders to other worlds quietly disappeared from the bookshelves. Tales that intimated a belief in God or gods or in anything invisible were destroyed. Any tale, ancient or modern, that extolled originality was forbidden.

New tales were encouraged. New myths were created by the most highly decorated artists of the land. To be like everyone else was the highest distinction a citizen could hope for. All the new myths promoted this ideal. Uniqueness, individuality, curiosity, became invidious qualities. They made enemies of the state. Anyone who stood out in some way was suspect. To be different was to condemn your fellow citizens. Those who were tall learnt to walk with a stoop. The intelligent learnt to be foolish.

It didn't take long before the old myths vanished. The old fairy tales were forgotten. Children were taught the new tales, the new versions, and didn't know any different. Those who were older had to re-acquaint themselves with the new versions. They didn't notice the subtle shift in tone.

By this means, without doing anything visible, the water that people drank, the water of understanding, was radically altered.

15

Nobody knew where the question-askers came from. The most advanced forms of surveillance had failed to reveal them spraying their question everywhere.

Elaborate plots to catch them had also failed. Spies could not find their network, or penetrate their groups. It was as if they didn't exist.

Posters offering information about them yielded nothing.

Neighbours denounced neighbours they didn't like or thought were acting suspiciously, but torture failed to yield confessions. It seemed incredible to the authorities that no one knew anything about the question-askers. It seemed equally incredible that the populace would shield them in any way.

For the first time the authorities began to harbour doubts about the populace. It had therefore been decided that everyone would be spied upon, that everyone would be placed under surveillance. The most sophisticated devices for spying on people had been deployed.

This posed a problem. It became clear that the people spying on the populace had themselves to be thoroughly trustworthy and there seemed no foolproof way of ensuring this.

16

Mirababa had dived in and emerged wet and exhilarated and perplexed. The voice had said 'Go in'. He had gone in and was now wet and shivering.

The moon was no longer clear on the surface of the lake. He sat and waited a long time. He watched till the moon returned to the surface of the water. Watching the moon made him drowsy. Before he knew it, he was asleep.

When he woke up he found one of the bards standing in front of him.

'Did you see anything?' the bard asked.

'No.'

'Did you hear anything?'

'I heard a voice.'

'What did it say?'

'It said "Go in."'

'What did you do?'

'I jumped into the lake.'

'Then what happened?'

'I got wet.'

'Did you learn anything from that?'

'Yes.'

'What?'

'That it was not the right thing to do.'

'What is the right thing to do?'

'I don't know.'

The old bard seemed satisfied. He retreated into the night, leaving the boy as perplexed as ever.

17

Karnak returned to the common field late the next evening, with the hope of seeing the question-askers again. The neighbouring streets were cordoned off as if it were a disaster area.

The streets were empty but the young lover sensed eyes everywhere. He walked as innocently as he could through an area he now felt teemed with spies. It felt like a trap.

He went towards the field. There were eyes in the trees, eyes in the grass, eyes behind hedges.

Evening had begun to fall. The muted noises began to give way to the silence which pervades the world before the screams are heard.

He didn't linger. He went on walking, trying not to think about all that was pressing on him to be thought about. He could not avoid thinking about the girl he loved, whom he had lost.

18

They revised the original myth about the prison. The world was not a prison. It was a garden. In the beginning man was placed in the garden. He had charge of the earth and all that was above and below it. The garden was the world and man was born a gardener. But one day man fell in love with an idea, and out of that idea came the beauty of woman.

The garden now had everything they needed, except for one thing. This one thing led to man and woman's unhappiness. They conceived the idea of freedom and ate from the tree of originality, and were thrown out of the garden into the fury of history.

In the revised version, man and woman have been slowly working their way back to the grandeur of their beginnings. The new ideology is the way. The authorities are the guardians. Obedience is the key. Dedication to the ideals of society is the route by which the original garden will be recovered.

But never again must the citizen think of freedom. Never again must they want to be different. The way to paradise lies in being like everyone else. The secret of happiness lies in doing what one is told.

This myth was recounted in many different stories. The variations only served to highlight the unchanging core. In books, comics, digital games, on television and on the radio, and through all the means of telepathic broadcasts, this revision of the myth was disseminated.

Philosophers elaborated on its ethical value. Using the myth's infinite applicability, scientists proved the Hierarchy's version of the future was inevitable. The new myth penetrated every level of society, into all deeds, all teachings.

No one knew that it was possible to ask questions. The people had forgotten how to ask questions.

19

Mirababa stayed by the lake in his wet clothes. He watched the moon in the water. In the space between watching the surface of the water and watching the moon he paid attention to what he felt, what he sensed. Sometimes he dreamt a strange dream in the lucidity of his gaze. He dreamt with his eyes wide open. What he dreamt eluded him. He wondered whether he had dreamt or whether he had seen.

The night did not seem to change. The moon did not seem to alter. He noticed the forest noises, the bird cries, the whistles, hoots, the wind among the trees. He heard footsteps coming towards him. They never arrived. Words drifted past him disembodied. He studied the glimmer of the false moon in the lake and the shining blackness of the water. None of it changed. Even the forest stayed the same.

The stars did not move. They were listening or watching. But the wind changed, blowing now one way, now another, making the earth hiss and the trees whistle.

Sometimes the boy thought he heard his grandfather's voice reading aloud from the ancient book of the original myths. He felt the old man's death keenly in those moments when his presence seemed to be in the wind. Snatches of words reached him.

'Go in… find what we have been seeking… share it with the world… go beyond…'

Mirababa stared into the darkness with a new sense of awareness, as though he were in mortal danger.

20

Those who smiled did not smile any less because the world had changed. They read the new versions of the old myths with irony. They read them with humour.

Apart from the pleasure they took in reading the new versions, there was no way of separating the ones who smiled from those who did not smile.

There was another difference between these two kinds of people. Those who smiled, smiled inwardly. Those who did not smile, smiled outwardly. This distinction was too subtle for the authorities.

There was a further distinction. But this required access to everyone's privacy, even their interiority. And while the authorities contemplated this as a possibility in the future, even perhaps a necessity, they had not yet developed the technology needed for such secret and inward surveillance.

Here was the real difference between these two kinds of people. Those who did not smile read the revised myths seriously, solemnly, importantly. Those who smiled read them with hidden laughter.

21

Karnak made the finding of the question-askers one of the chief missions of his life. After catching glimpses of them in the field at night, he often returned there with the hope of seeing them again. But he saw only the increasing presence of the police.

It didn't occur to him that people wanted by the authorities never returned to the same place. He fell into the same superstitious thinking as the police, expecting the question-askers to repeat themselves.

After returning fruitlessly to the field several times, he began to think as people do who have failed in a quest. He began to think that the question-askers did not exist. He began to think he had imagined them. Seeing something once was not enough to make him believe. He needed to see them again before he could believe.

But he went on seeking the question-askers. He thought of them as an underground group. Their elusiveness made them mythical. Being unable to find them made him demote the uniqueness of his experience.

When the newspapers referred to them as an urban myth, the young lover, being inexperienced, believed what the newspapers said. The effect of this was to diminish his hopes.

He had lost his lover without resistance and now the object of his quest was proving an illusion.

22

How do you find people who do not want to be found? How do you find people who have made themselves so invisible that they have become an urban myth?

Karnak exhausted all attempts at finding them. He prowled all manner of streets at dusk. He scoured the newspapers, seeking clues. He listened to conversations with a double mind. He saw hints everywhere, but the hints were enigmas. Like everyone else he saw the legends painted in big black letters on the walls of the city.

WHO IS THE WATCHER?

This made him feel that he was being watched by invisible omnipresent eyes. Images of giant cyclopean eyes appeared on pavements, on government buildings, on billboards, on the sides of lorries, on long stretches of walls. Square bits of paper fluttered down the streets. On them were images of prison bars with a solitary face, images of a single luminous eye, or simply the words:

WHO IS THE PRISONER?

People did not pick up these flyers, but it was impossible not to see the images or the words at a single glance. Karnak picked up a few of these flyers, as discreetly as possible, and studied them for clues. They gave no information of any kind. They had no other signs on them. The young lover was convinced that their neutrality held a clue, if only he could decipher it.

He noticed that as soon as the flyers floated down the streets they were cleared away by figures in white whose express job was the elimination of anything dangerous to the state.

Karnak grew frustrated. As he had nowhere to turn for information or hope, he decided one day to try something he had never thought of before.

23

It was the worst time of the night. Mirababa had been sitting on the bank of the lake. He was fine; he had made an accommodation with his perplexity. He had shivered in his wet clothes, but had grown used to the dampness. The moon hadn't moved from the centre of the lake. The stars hadn't moved in the sky.

He remembered tales his grandfather used to tell him of nights that lasted a week. He had heard about nights lengthened by the gods for their secret purposes. He had also heard tales about the time to come when night would descend on the world and stay forever. This had been the greatest fear of the people.

Tales of the never-ending night were seldom told and never told to children for fear of poisoning their minds. But sometimes when Mirababa slept he overheard those tales told at night when the old ones drank outside, under the eaves. They told stories about how the prison came to be. They spoke of the fall of their great ancestor, of the loss of his immortal white garment and his shining immortal spear made of the timeless elements of mercury, sulphur, and salt.

He heard tales of how this ancestor was once master of all creation, neither man nor woman, and higher than all the angels. He learnt how this ancestor, who conceived an immortal lust which broke the spell of his uniqueness, was put into a magic sleep from which he awoke into the prison of all nature. By his side was his mortal mate, that beautiful woman at the beginning of time, who might have been time itself.

The boy, in his sleep (for he was a light sleeper), heard snatches of these fantastic legends whispered by the old ones. It was this that awoke his interest in myths.

The night he heard the myth of the longest night to come was one of the most frightening of his life. He had nightmares about it for a week. He told his nightmares to his grandfather, who replied with this riddle:

'The longest night will end with the longest night.'

The boy had not understood. The grandfather said:

'An eternal night will descend on the world. But it will end.'

'How?'

'It will end when one person wakes up.'

'Wakes up from what?'

'From sleep.'

'Will we all be asleep?'

'Yes.'

'If we are asleep how will we know it is the longest night?'

'Because people will be asleep and yet awake.'

'How can that be?'

'It happens all the time.'

'Are we asleep now?'

'Yes.'

'But I'm awake. I'm talking to you.'

'How do you know you are awake?'

'Because I am. I can feel it. I can see you. I pinch myself and I feel it.'

'How do you know you're not doing all this in your dream?'

'I'm not dreaming, am I?'

'How do you know?'

'If everyone is asleep and awake, how can anyone wake up then?'

'By going in.'

'You've said that before.'

'I haven't.'

'Yes, you have.'

'I have never said this to you,' said the grandfather smiling. 'But I will say it to you again. Maybe you heard me say it to you in the future.'

'But how can I hear something said in the future?'

'You just did.'

The boy paused. The grandfather enjoyed the boy's perplexity. He seemed to want to increase it, as though perplexity were a desired state of mind.

'If someone wakes up, the eternal night will end?'

'Yes.'

'So everyone has to wake up to end the terrible night?'

'Yes, but the night is defeated by one person first. Then everyone else will follow.'

'And who will this person be?'

'It could be anyone. It could be a child, a mad man, a

woman, a girl, a lover, a thief, a tyrant, a jailor, a storyteller, a shoemaker, a poet, or a whore.'

'What is a whore?'

'You will find out soon enough.'

The boy paused again.

'How will this person wake up?'

'By going in.'

'You've said that before.'

'Ah, this is one future you heard.'

'How will they go in?'

It was the old man's turn to pause. He had a troubled look on his face. Then with a new voice, the voice of fear and wonder, he said:

'By being the first to escape from this prison that has been our home from the beginning of time.'

The boy remembered this conversation as he sat by the lake. The round moon shone in its centre. It had been a long night.

24

In search of clues Karnak decided to go into the beautiful building with the sky-piercing spire. It was a simple building with a triangular pediment and fine elegant columns.

He had often been taken there as a child. Often he'd fallen asleep during the sermon. Though it was required by tradition, he hadn't been there for many years. He could not remember why he stopped going.

He had always admired the building, even when hurrying past it on his way to work. It occurred to him that the people there might be able to help him.

It was a particularly fine morning. The sunlight was tender on the trees. He found the church almost empty. Three people were seated at great distances from one another. The service was just about to begin. He took a seat at the front, and resolved not to fall asleep as he had done when he was a child.

Figures in white vestments made their way to the front and performed a ritual in a language he did not know and made signs in the air. There was a table covered in a white cloth with gold borders. One of the men held a golden cup. Another spoke of blood turned into wine. A woman in a white surplice talked of the original garden and the fall and the first sin and salvation. An unseen choir sang. Their voices were beautiful. The man who had spoken about wine prayed on behalf of everyone. Then he asked if anyone present wanted to drink of the wine. None of the three people moved. He said something about confessing sins. No one came forward. One of the officials made a sign. Another drank from the cup, another ate of the bread. The myth of the garden was read out from a huge book with golden letters. It was the new version of the ancient myth. The choir of boys sang again. When it was all over Karnak was asleep in the pew, along with the three others who had attended the service.

It was the best sleep he'd had in a long time.

Once she said to him:

    'I think I am the most ordinary person in the world.'

    He laughed.

    'You? Ordinary? There's nothing ordinary about you.'

    'But there is. That's all I want.'

    'To be ordinary?'

    'Yes. It's the hardest thing in our times to be ordinary.'

    'I'm not sure I follow you. What do you mean by ordinary?'

    'Someone who loves simply, like a child.'

    'That's not ordinary. That's beautiful.'

    'Someone who wants this world to end.'

    'Why would you want that?'

    'Someone who likes watching things grow.'

    'That's not ordinary. That's just old-fashioned.'

    'Someone who can be loved by you.'

    'Does my love make you feel ordinary?'

    'Yes, and I love it.'

    'Your love makes me feel drunk. You have the strangest beauty. Sometimes just looking at you makes me feel like I'm hallucinating. Sometimes I feel I'm going to fall. Sometimes just looking at you gives me panic attacks.'

    'But why?'

    'I think I would die if I lose you. I think I would just quietly go mad.'

    'Why do you think you would lose me?'

'When you really love, it's your first fear.'

'When you really love you know you can never lose that person. Even if they got taken to another world.'

'Please don't make any hints like that. I can't bear it.'

'But it's true, though. How can you lose what you love?'

'Because it won't be there any more.'

'So you agree about absences?'

'Your absence would make the world die.'

'If only that were true.'

'Without your beauty this world is empty. It will be a desert.'

'You're back to beauty again. You know what I think about beauty.'

'I know and I don't agree. There's nothing wrong with beauty. It's the charm of life.'

'Beauty in the eye is blindness in the soul.'

'Did you make that up?'

'Maybe, or maybe I read it somewhere.'

'Let's not talk about books.'

'Books books books.'

'In that case, your beauty makes the air shine. It makes the world stand still. Every time I look at you my heart jumps and everything becomes unreal. You know there are moments when I look at you and I turn around and weep. Your beauty…'

'Every time you talk about my beauty it makes me ill.'

'But why?'

Amalantis paused. She went into a deep thought for a while, and never gave an answer.

25

By a stroke of genius, and wholly by accident, the authorities found a way to uncover those who collaborated with the question-askers.

An individual was hauled into a police station. He had been hanging about a suspicious area at night. During questioning he revealed something strange. He did not hear the screams at night. From this it was reasoned, by the sages of the land, that those who didn't hear the screams didn't hear them because they were also screaming. It followed that those who heard the screams were not screaming while they slept. If they did not scream at night then they were not normal. They were not like everyone else. They must have bad consciences, or evil thoughts. They might also be awake. And if they were awake while everyone else was sleeping, what on earth were they doing?

This was how the authorities came upon the method for detecting those harbouring thoughts dangerous to the state. The Sleep Police went from house to house in the dead of night listening out for those who did not scream while they slept.

26

The church had subtly altered its doctrines. All mention of the earliest myths of the prison were quietly dropped. The old books revealing the primeval myth of the prison were hidden away. The new bibles replaced the myth of the first prison with that of the first garden. But the rest of the story was retained.

After the garden there was still the fall. In some versions there was a long period in the desert and then there was the wasteland. The generation raised on the myth of the prison got confused by the story of the garden. The generation raised on the myth of the garden wondered how they got to the garden and wondered if there was a way back. People were taught not to ask exactly where the garden was. Historians were encouraged not to speculate about its precise location.

Then the populace was educated to treat the stories in the bible not as stories any more, but as truths. They were events that really happened long ago. In this way the promises made in the book of a future garden in which all would be happy seemed more likely to come true.

Some philosophers maintained that the garden is everywhere. The past, present, and future are all gardens. They urged their fellow citizens to regard life with more wonder.

The churches grew emptier. Services were held to empty pews.

27

Then one morning a curious word appeared in the world. It could be seen on walls, billboards, on sides of lorries and cars, and spray-painted on the streets. Leaflets fluttering in the breeze bore this single word. People hurrying to work after a night of sleep-screaming were perplexed by the word.

The word was strange, not because it was unknown, but because it was an illogical paradoxical thought. The word implied its opposite. But if its opposite was true then how could anyone be aware of the word?

The authorities descended on the streets and destroyed all the leaflets bearing the single harmless-seeming word. Walls were thoroughly scrubbed. They need not have bothered. The word barely registered in people's minds. When it did it was with a sense of bemusement.

It turned out to be a normal day. It was a day of light breezes and intermittent sunshine. It was like any other day in a world where the water had changed. But that night people screamed louder in their sleep. All over the cities these screams could be heard. They were like the lonely debris washed home from a day of living in the world.

But there were isolated dreamers who, in their sleep, said one word over and over again.

That word was:

Upwake!

28

A rumour went round the underworld that people who did not scream in their sleep were being arrested. Small children had been taken away to the immense land of eternal darkness. Young girls were woken in the depth of the night and quietly removed to pale white vans, their helpless parents forlorn on doorsteps. One or two state philosophers, working late into the night, found themselves abandoned in the desert of darkness, with its soundlessly sleeping corpses. One or two priests were rounded up and delivered to the grim warehouse of eternal night.

It didn't take long for fake screamers to join the real screamers. They could be coached if they were not real screamers. In some houses machines with recorded wails did the job. The authorities couldn't tell the difference between the real and the false.

After a while it was realised that mistakes had been made. Huge financial compensations were made in secret to families who lost innocent children. Plaques commemorated missing priests. The vanished state philosopher became, in absentia, an icon of contemporary thought, his works made compulsory study at the universities.

Before he was taken away, the philosopher had been working on a new idea. He had been nourishing the theme of his great tome for most of his life. After years of contributing to the altered myth of the prison, he had a strange revelation. He found a flaw in the original myth. The authorities were delighted by his discovery and encouraged him to make his findings public. The book which he had been working on, written in longhand in black notebooks, deep into the night, was called: *The Universe is My Dream and Mis-representation*.

Its thesis was simple: the human mechanism, fatally flawed, misperceives reality. Man may as well be in a dream. Enlightened guardians are needed to lead humanity out of the forest of illusions into a brilliant new future. The senses cannot be corrected. But the mind, through suitable myths, can exert a corrective to the parallax of the sensorium.

It was a book written in aphorisms. Some were dense, others lapidary. All were designed to strengthen the notion that society needs strong leaders, that people cannot trust their senses, and that enlightened myth is the true guide of the mind.

Here are some of his aphorisms:

– That you see a star in the night sky does not mean that the star sees you. The universe does not mirror consciousness. Consciousness mirrors the universe.

– Those who sleep, awake; those who wake up, sleep.

– Society is the journey of myth through the reality of being.

– Those who yearn for power create more sleep.

– Words serve to reduce reality. Words are not things.

– To misperceive is natural to man. Philosophy and myth correct the defective vision of nature.

– Gods are the invention of man; our gods mirror us. When the gods die we are without reflections projected into the infinite.

– The old society invented gods out of the rigorous necessity of metaphor. Metaphors, once they assume human form, take on a life of their own, like the clay figures breathed on by the Demiurge that is us.

– We made the gods in our image.

– The death of God is the beginning of man.

– A peerless light shines from the original myth, but words stain its purity.

– Man was not born in prison, but prison was born in man.

– The original prison was the original garden: we have cultivated our myth.

30

Those were some of his aphorisms, written at different times, scattered across several folios. He was, however, working on an extended aphorism when the knock sounded on the door. His last thought, unfinished, was in fact a meditation on the word that had appeared everywhere that day:

– To wake up is paradoxical. If you are awake, there is no waking up from wakefulness. If you are asleep, you cannot be awake enough to know you are asleep. Consequently the word *Upwake* is futile. Revolutionaries are seldom philosophers. This is just as well. If the word *Upwake* is meant to destabilise the state, peaceful sleep is assured for generations to come. To wake up those who are asleep you must first either wake them up or make them know they are asleep. Consequently you must speak to them in their dreams. There are only two things that can speak to a sleeping person: dreams or myth, which is a kind of dream. If I were a revolutionary I would work on the kingdom of sleep, the theatre of intimate listening. The conscious mind has limitations; the subconscious has none. This is the limitation of philosophy: we address only the conscious mind. A note for the Hierarchy: exercise power over sleep. The psychiatrist should do the work of the state. Psychonalysts should report their findings to the state. The greatest leader would first be a master of the dreams of the peop...

Then came the fatal knock.

31

Among those arrested for not screaming in their sleep was a comedian, one of the funniest people in the land, and a darling of the establishment.

On this particular night the comedian was working on a series of jokes for an upcoming show. He had chosen, as his subject for the show, the not very funny question-askers. He thought it ludicrous that words painted on walls could have any impact on anyone. He had been wanting, for some time now, to take a crack at the different words that appeared every day, words that bewildered people and upset the authorities. Somehow he had never been able to find a way to make comedy out of them.

He couldn't make fun of the myth of the original prison. It was too serious a subject. Almost sacred. He knew this, but as the best loved and most famous comedian in the land he had been urged many times to contribute to efforts to calm the public mood. This day's word seemed perfect for mockery. He had sketched a few lines already.

– 'Can you imagine being asleep and someone puts a "wakeup" sign over your face? Do they expect you to read it while you are snoring?'

– 'So there I am, having this dream about this gorgeous girl. Then this guy in a balaclava sticks a sign that says "wake-up" in my face. Do you think I'd notice?'

– 'These people who put up all those words, what do you think their life is like? They get up in the morning and they spend all day thinking of one word. "Goose!" No, that won't do. What about "Leg!" No, maybe not. Oh I know. "Eat!" People need to eat. We should tell people what they know already. No message is more powerful than an obvious message, right? What about "Walk!" Now people don't know how to do that. I tell you what gets me. What gets me is why do they choose one word? Why not a whole sentence? Why not a whole manifesto? Whatever happened to the good old days of powerful slogans? Workers of the world and all that. Do you think these guys have got so small from hiding in little cubby holes underground that they can only think up one word at a time?'

The comedian was pleased with the tone. He could see himself in front of the crowd already. He could imagine their anticipation and surprise as he began to tear the word of the day apart.

The roaring belly laughs, the creased up faces and the shaking bellies, the anonymous laughter from the Hierarchy boxes never failed to fill him with pleasure. He was a master of humour. He knew how to create waves of laughter from one side of the audience which would rise to meet the waves from the other side in a volcanic eruption of hilarity. This would be his biggest success.

He had begun to laugh in anticipation, when the fatal knock sounded.

32

Refreshed by his sleep, Karnak came to the conclusion that the priests would not be able to help him in his quest.

He wandered the streets, looking for clues to the identity of the mysterious people who appeared and disappeared, leaving words and leaflets and mayhem behind.

As he wandered, it occurred to him that the solution might lie in affinities. Who were most like the question-askers? Who did they most resemble? The answer came to him almost immediately. It was obvious. He wondered why he had never thought of it before. The people who were most like the question-askers were the artists. He would seek them out. They might give him clues, throw light on his search.

To his surprise artists were not hard to find. They seemed to be everywhere, once he started looking. Striking posters for exhibitions were up in all the shop windows. Retrospectives were advertised in all the newspapers. There were interviews with artists in Sunday magazines. They were everywhere. The difficulty was which one to choose. One seemed as radical as the other, and all were doing outlandish things. There seemed no limit to what art could be. One artist declared everything to be a work of art, including the shirt on her back. Another claimed that just a look of his turned anything into a work of art.

After thinking about it for some time, Karnak decided

he would just go into the first exhibition he saw advertised. He went in and found a big crowd of people, drinking and talking all at once. It was not clear who anyone was talking to. Some just seemed to be talking to the air.

They were a well-dressed crowd, but they looked harassed and strained. Karnak was struck by their curious energy. He also took in the many framed and not framed pictures on the walls, the curious objects in niches, on plinths, or projecting out of the walls. Some peculiar object swung from the ceiling. It looked like a stone pendulum.

No one in the crowd was looking at any of the pictures or objects. But Karnak went round and looked. The pictures were very straightforward images of life in the city. There were people in bars, at the theatre, at a comedy show. There was a child in a dry field, a tropical sunset, a landscape in France. There were canal scenes in Venice, rooftops in Lagos. All were painted in bright bold colours. Karnak went from one picture to another, feeling no need to linger. Each picture gave all of its information at once.

As he was moving away from a Syrian landscape, he heard a voice over his shoulder:

'Do you always look so quickly?'

He turned and saw a man in his early thirties, with a confident look on his fresh face, and doubt in his hollow eyes.

'I don't look at pictures much.'

'Oh. Why not?'

'I'm not trained.'

'Do you think you need training to look at art?'

'I don't know. I suppose it's a specialisation.'

'Specialisation?'

'Yes.'

'It's art.'

'Really?' Karnak said, looking nervously at the paintings.

'You don't think so?'

'I don't know what art is.'

'You're looking at it,' the man with doubt in his eyes said. 'Who are you?'

'Me?'

'What are you doing here? Who invited you?'

'I wanted to speak to the artist…'

'Are you from a newspaper?'

'Newspaper?'

Karnak had hardly comprehended the turn the conversation was taking when he felt a fist on his face. It was more like a slap, but it surprised him. Before he could react there were many voices in his ears and large faces looming up at him and mouths speaking or shouting. He could not make out anything they said. He found himself at the door, and a shove sent him flying into the street. He staggered back, but regained his balance. The door slammed behind him.

The artist of that show, he decided, could not throw light on anything for him.

33

He walked round and round in a daze. So much perplexed him. He tried to think but all he wanted to think about eluded him, so he went on walking till he found himself near a park. Across the road he saw another gallery and went over. It was another exhibition with another party in progress. He could see the crowd through the windows. They seemed more mature. He went in and, deciding to be more practical, set about finding the artist.

Again no one was looking at the pictures on the walls. The objects scattered about the place, flotsam from the sea after a storm, were also entirely ignored. The place was packed so tight that just smiling increased the sense of constriction. Everyone was talking. The roar of voices made Karnak feel slightly deaf. So many faces close up made him dizzy. He weaved in mild delirium through the crush of bodies and churn of voices.

It was impossible to tell who the artist might be among the elegant guests. He tried asking, but the noise drowned him out. Someone thrust a drink into his hand. Finding that he could not speak, he decided he might as well look at the pictures.

These were different. He couldn't make out anything in them whatsoever, just shapes and a mass of colours. The canvasses were huge, their frames heavy, some of bronze, some of wood. Even when he looked closer at the paintings he could not make out what the shapes were, nor could he determine the colours. This must be what they called art.

He was musing in this way when a grey-haired man spoke to him.

'You are the only one here looking at the paintings. I noticed it at once.'

'Did you?'

'You look as if you understand them.'

'I understand nothing.'

'Is that a philosophy?'

'No.'

'These days,' said the grey-haired man, 'everything is a philosophy, just as everything is art.'

'Is everything art?'

'So they say.'

'Really?'

'So we are told.'

'What are we told?'

'That there are no distinctions between one person and another, that one is as much a philosopher as the next man, as much an artist as the next. That's what we are told. There's more, but I'm too drunk to remember.'

'Is it true?'

'How would I know? I'm an old man, I repeat what I'm told. You're young, of the new school. What do you think?'

'Think?'

'Yes.'

'Thinking is dangerous.'

'Do you think so – ha ha, forgive the pun. But do you?'

'Yes.'

'Do you like danger?'

'Not really.'

'What are you doing here then?'

'Is it dangerous here?'

'Do you feel in danger?'

'No.'

'That's disappointing.'

'Why?'

'If I had my youth again I would only do dangerous things.'

'How do you mean?'

'Not the obvious things like taking drugs, driving too fast, climbing Everest. I mean, the really dangerous things.'

'Like what?'

'Thinking for myself.'

'Don't you do that already?'

'Nobody does. No one has done it for over a hundred years. We've all forgotten how to think. It's all done for us. Fashion is chosen for us. Art is chosen for us. When there were books, they were decided for us. We've forgotten what it's like to have a mind of our own. Most people don't even know what a mind is.'

'Are you the artist?'

'Good heavens, no. Why do you say that?'

'You sound like one.'

'Are you mad? Artists are the most unthinking people, the state's best kept secrets. They are machines for giving us shocks that can be sold. No one reads the mood of what is needed to create a harmless scandal better than the artists of our times. In the old days we had coliseums, today we have artists. They're the new merchant class, rich as Croesus, every one of them. They dream of nothing else. No, my young friend, the artist is the new banker. I am certainly not an artist, and I consider it an insult that you think me one.'

'If you're not the artist, who are you?'

'I –' said the grey-haired gentleman, drawing himself up to his fullest height, 'I am the last man in the world who knows…'

At that moment a young woman in fur and a low-cut dress appeared and led the grey-haired man away.

'I had to rescue you,' he heard her say sweetly, 'from that fan…'

Karnak stood a while. No one else spoke to him. Without touching his drink, he left the exhibition and wandered the lonely roads.

34

He had been walking aimlessly for some time when a large car drew up smoothly alongside him. Karnak walked faster, fearing that he was being followed, that the authorities were onto him. But the car kept pace with him. He was about to break into a run, when a tinted window was lowered and a voice called out. He staggered backwards in panic. Then he saw a face calmly looking up at him.

With a mild imperious movement of the palm, the grey-haired man summoned him over. The windows slid back up, reflecting the louring sky. The back door opened and, after a pause, Karnak got in.

In the back seat, with the grey-haired man, sat the beautiful woman he had seen earlier. She had her palm on the gentleman's upper thigh and she regarded Karnak with an ironic smile. It was a smile that crooked a little upwards to the right of her face. Her eyes were cold and green and bright.

'Sit down, dear boy, we were unceremoniously separated,' he said. 'I was enjoying our conversation. You wanted to meet the artist. Fancy taking me for the artist.' He gave the woman an appalled look. 'We are on our way to see one of the most famous artists of our day. Perhaps I should say of our minute.'

Karnak looked lost.

'He chose to have his exhibition on the same day as a hundred other artists knowing that everyone would go to his. We are going to pay court to Maecenas himself. You know who I mean, don't you? No? It doesn't matter. Sit back, and let's talk about all the things I would do if I had your youth again.'

Karnak sat very still and straight, conscious of the eyes of the woman on him. The car sped on through streets he did not recognise. He was trying to work out where he was when, to his surprise, the woman began speaking. She had a voice quite out of harmony with her beauty, a see-saw, sing-song voice.

'It is hard to be truly dangerous when you're young,' she said, looking at the older man. 'One hardly knows what one is doing. I think your age is the best time to be dangerous.'

'You make me sound ancient.'

'Not ancient, just the right age to be dangerous.'

'I'm intrigued.'

'I should like to be deadly at your age.'

'What a charming thought. But at my age, I have everything to lose. At yours you have nothing to lose but illusions.'

'Illusions are the most precious things,' the woman said.

'Do you think so? I think the opposite. I think having no illusions is the most perfect state of mind.'

'I like illusions. I like men who still have their illusions intact.' She looked fixedly at Karnak, then she wriggled, and turned back to the grey-haired gentleman.

'What dangerous things would you do if you had your youth again?'

'First of all, I would learn to think clearly and take nothing for granted. Secondly, I would be in love all the time. If I couldn't find someone to love, I would love the future. I would love the trees, I would love difficulties, I would love the edges of things. Thirdly...'

And so the Rolls-Royce rolled on down the road, speeding towards adventure. The young lover, bashful under the sceptical gaze of beauty, kept silent, and something about the older man's voice mesmerised him. He didn't notice when the man stopped talking. The older man and the woman were staring at him.

'You didn't answer our question.'

He looked blank.

'What are you doing now that is dangerous?' the woman said.

'Me?'

He felt himself coming out in a sweat.

'Being in this car with you.'

The grey-haired man smiled mysteriously. No one spoke after that until the car drew to a halt and the chauffeur opened the doors. Ornate metal gates swung open and they climbed marble steps up to a garden with three fountains made of gold. Beyond the garden was a mansion of unspeakable magnificence. Uniformed servants opened doors that led to golden interiors where golden lions sat in monumental tranquillity. They were led through many halls with gold-leaf ceilings and vast tapestries on the walls and doors brought from antique kingdoms. The place was a museum of ancient artefacts and modern acquisitions. Then at last, after wandering round the labyrinths of the imponderable grounds, they arrived at the central hall.

Seated on a golden throne was a stocky man with an air of distilled ennui. He gave the impression of one who has seen everything and seen through everyone. Karnak surmised he was in his mid-forties. He had a haughty bearing and a permanent fixture on his face was a faintly contemptuous smile.

'Here is the artist of our time,' said the grey-haired man, as they drew closer. 'The rest are mere aspirants.'

Around them in the vast hall was an unimaginable collection of molluscs, ropes, fishes in bowls, heads of animals, eyeballs in a frame, a canvas that combined a shoe with a landscape, broken violins, a colour-spraying apparatus, a miniature windmill, a blown-up picture of the most famous comedian in the land, the collected works of the recently deified national philosopher, torn-up canvasses, a recent dinner framed in polystyrene hanging from the ceiling, a half-stuffed dog in a shrunken pool, chandeliers, gold spoons, a table longer than a tennis court, and probably the most expensive car in the world, parked in a corner of the hall.

The artist barely stirred at the grey-haired man's greeting. It was as though nothing in the world could touch him, impregnable as he was in the fortress of his fame.

35

The moon was still in the middle of the lake. Mirababa moved in and out of sleep. After a while he could not distinguish sleep from waking. He knew he had to keep awake but he didn't know what he was keeping awake for.

He had to keep vigil.

There were times when the moon wavered in the centre of the lake, or when it grew fainter, or when it blazed in whiteness. There were times when it did not appear to be there. The forest all around breathed out a potent darkness. There were times when the boy thought he saw demons emerging from the depths of the forest.

A single thought kept hammering away in his head. KEEP AWAKE KEEP AWAKE KEEP AWAKE. He was finding it difficult.

There was a moment he imagined that a girl rose out of the lake and came and sat next to him. She was silent for a long while. When he turned to look at her he noticed that she was not wet. Her skin glowed as if she had swallowed the moon. She had a strange smile on her face, as if she expected him to notice something obvious but didn't. When he looked back at the lake he was surprised to find it wasn't there.

'What's happened to the lake?' asked Mirababa.

'What lake?'

'There was a lake here. Now it's gone.'

'Never has there been a lake here.'

Mirababa looked again. He saw there wasn't even a moon, not above, not below.

'And what happened to the moon?'

'What moon?'

'There was a bright moon in the middle of the lake.'

'There hasn't been a moon tonight. It's been dark all night.'

The boy was silent. It occurred to him that the girl knew something he didn't.

'Who are you?'

'That's the first question you should have asked me.'

'Why?'

'Because the first question is the most important question.'

'Why?'

'Because it determines all the questions you ask after that.'

'Why?'

'Because questions have their own logic.'

'What was wrong with my first question?'

'You asked about something that was not there.'

'What's wrong with that?'

'If you are more interested in something that is not there rather than in something that is there, then you are not interested in what is there. Then sooner or later it will not be there any more.'

'But the lake was there.'

'No, it wasn't.'

'How do you know?'

'How do you know?'

'Because I've been looking at it all night. I even jumped into it.'

'Then why is it not there now?'

'I don't know.'

'If you don't know why it's not there, then how do you know it was there?'

'I don't know.'

'Do you know anything?'

The strange smile had returned to the girl's face.

'No, I don't think I do,' he said, after a pause.

'Not anything?'

'I don't know.'

'What do you know right now?'

'Right now?'

'This very moment.'

'I think I know I am talking to you.'

'Do you know it or not?'

Mirababa paused again and considered. Was he talking to her or not? While he was thinking about it he was silent. He wasn't talking any more.

'No, I don't think I'm talking to you,' he said, and realised he was talking to her.

'Yes, I'm talking to you,' he corrected.

'How do you know?'

'How do I know?'

'Do you have to repeat the question?'

'Yes.'

'Why?'

'Because I say it to myself.'

'Didn't you hear it in the first place?'

'I hear it better when I say it to myself.'

'So how do you know you're talking to me?'

'I can hear your voice. I can hear my voice. I'm here. You're here.'

'Am I here?'

The boy looked at her again. He became aware of her strangeness.

'You're right,' he said, in a softened voice. 'My first question was the wrong question.'

'Why do you say that?'

'Because of that wrong first question, I haven't been able to ask you the question I really wanted to ask.'

'What question is that?'

'Who are you?'

'You've asked that already.'

'I asked it at the wrong time. It was part of other questions.'

Mirababa paused and took a deep breath. He turned to the girl. He noticed how beautiful she had become.

'Can I begin again?'

'Not really.'

'Can't we pretend?'

'All right,' the girl said, brightening. 'Let's pretend to begin again. First shut your eyes. Imagine everything is at the beginning. You have to alter time. Can you do that? You have to imagine everything as it was. If you can do that then we can begin again.'

'I'll try,' Mirababa said meekly.

'Are you ready?'

The boy shut his eyes. Fervently, he tried to imagine everything as it was at the beginning.

36

Karnak sat in an upholstered armchair the colour of money. The grey-haired gentleman and the woman sat next to him, on a pure white sofa. A butler in a white uniform placed drinks on a diamond-shaped table.

The artist had begun speaking as soon as they sat down. He spoke from his throne of gold, as if continuing what he was saying a moment before. He spoke as if to an unchanging audience. He spoke in a manner that made Karnak feel that he was not there. Karnak felt himself as an absence, a sort of a ghost, there and not there.

'I don't care much for people's opinions,' the artist was saying. 'I make opinions. No one can create my world. I see the artist as the true king. People pay us to make up the world. If the artist is a true artist, the best thing he does is create the most important thing in society. In the olden days that was beauty, or religion, or myth. But we are modern and we are bored with beauty, we are sick of religion, and we've sorted out the old myths. God left us a long time ago. The most significant force in society is not what it used to be. Not that long ago, fame was the new religion. To be famous was to be a kind of god. The greatest artist then was the most famous artist. But we've done fame. We've come to the end of fame. It's too easy to be famous. Every idiot artist is famous now. Fame has got devalued because there's just too much of it. Fame used to be magic. You could conjure with it. You could be a mountain in people's minds. You could be a demon or a monster. Now fame makes you tame, makes you common. Nothing more commonplace than fame.'

He paused, not to look at them, but to scratch his cheek. He had paused because he felt like pausing. There was no reason for it. In just the same way, he began again, arbitrarily, as if speaking were his sublime prerogative and hearing was that of his listeners.

'We've gone beyond fame. We've done the Everest of fame. Fame belongs to the past. Deliberately not being famous is the new fame. I declare it so. No artist conquers again what has already been conquered. They do something new. They find a new territory. If the artist is true they will create what is most important in their times. It is not the work that the artist creates that counts. It is the value that the artist creates that counts. All else is bilge. Being a great artist is easy. It's been done several times. Being great is boring. Too many people have done it. But have you noticed that the really great artists create the notion of their greatness separate from the notion of their works? They create a new value. Anyone can create a great work. But how many have created a new value? The really great artist creates a new value. This new value is their true work of art. The works they are known for are merely justifications, objective correlatives, coins to make an idea concrete. In a way you don't need the work of art any more. You can just create a new value. That would be greater than any work.'

At the movement of a finger someone appeared from behind an arras and poured him liquid from a golden goblet into an emerald cup. He gulped it all down in one.

'The question is this: what is the most important value of our times? What is the most important symbol? I'll tell you. It's simple. It's all around. Cities are made of it, civilisations are sustained by it, religions need it, pyramids are erected with it. Long have we looked right through it while it shapes our lives. Artists have created all manner of things, but never has an artist created this value, with this symbol. For the first time in human history an artist has sculpted at last with this magic value, painted with it, drawn with it, and used it as the primal force in his art, the chief idiom of his work. Great bankers have created vast edifices of power with it. Merchants have funded whole eras of art with its power. Kings and Popes have used it. But I am the first and the only one so far to have created this value entirely in itself. I am the first artist of money.'

He paused and looked upward.

'The rest merely seek it, lust after it, charge high prices for their work to get it, but not one of them has created money as the chief and only value of their art. Money is the most important force of our times. The person who masters money masters society. The artist who masters money masters the future. No longer is there religion. There is only the art of money, its temples, its altars, its apotheoses, its mountain peaks, its dreams. These I celebrate. These I create. The rest is folly.'

The artist paused again, and looked around the vast hall. With a melancholy sweep of the hand, he said:

'Money is the new imagination. The genie of our age, from the magic lamp of our times, is money. It is the only reliable open sesame. To mint money is primitive; to incarnate money is genius. Why has no one thought of it before? Money sends our thoughts round the world. Money is the new Mona Lisa, its smile more mysterious and seductive. People are interested in my works not because they see art, but because they see money. I have compelled money and art to get into bed with each other. It is the new alchemy. Turning lead into gold – that is too laborious and quaint. But turning anything I look at into money, now that is the new alchemy. Midas had to touch things to turn them into gold. I merely have to think of them and they are changed.'

As if he were alone in the vast hall, the artist pulled a face, then continued:

'I am yet to discover what the limits of money are. I see none. With money I have compelled destiny, altered fate, and coerced providence. With money I have erected a value more lasting than bronze and my immortality is more certain than the mountains. Beyond money where can you go? There is nothing beyond. Money is the last frontier of the imagination. It is the last object in art. Artists of the future have nowhere to go. There will be no new beginnings. I am the end of art.'

The artist spoke into the vast hall, his voice drifting round the columns, and disappearing towards the embossed ceiling. The lights dimmed and brightened mysteriously through the stained-glass windows.

Karnak, almost comatose now, turned to the grey-haired gentleman and the lady, who were both fast asleep on the sofa. The artist, addressing the hall with dull eyes, had not noticed.

Certain that he would get no clues here, the young lover crept out of the room. As he left he heard the artist begin speaking again.

He didn't wait to listen.

37

Mirababa was attempting to reverse time. He shut his eyes and tried to recreate the beginning. He tried to imagine the moment again when the girl, dripping moonlight, emerged from the lake. He imagined the moment so hard, he got lost in his imagining.

When he woke, it was a dark night. The lake shone in the middle of the forest and the moon shone in the middle of the lake. It was as though no time had passed at all.

He waited and watched. Nothing happened. The lake did not change, the moon did not move, and the darkness did not alter. It was as if time stood still. He could not even feel the wind.

It occurred to him that maybe he was dead. This was the world as the dead experienced it: the same scene before them eternally. If he was dead the thought didn't bother him. He found it rather pleasant. He played at being dead. Things would remain like this, unchanging, forever.

He decided that if the lake, with the moon, was always going to be there then he may as well get used to it. He stared at the moon in the lake. There was something odd about it. He had always assumed that the moon was a reflection. But the more he looked the more it became clear that it was real. This surprised him. He looked up at the sky, and saw that there was no moon up there at all.

The sky was very dark, though he could make out the stars.

It was odd that the moon was in the lake and not in the sky. Was he in an inverted universe?

He remembered the words of his grandfather. Go in. What did he mean? Mirababa had gone into the lake and had only got cold and wet. A girl had come to him from the lake and he had asked the wrong question. What was the right question? Why hadn't the girl come back?

Then in a flash a clear thought occurred to him.

'I have not been asking the right question.'

This was a little revelation. He sensed it was leading him somewhere. He said to himself:

'What is the right question?'

He thought about it. He stopped thinking. He became aware of the strangeness of his situation.

'What am I doing here?' he asked himself.

'And who am I anyway?'

The question intrigued him. He had never asked it before. This struck him as very odd.

'Why have I never asked this question before?'

He liked the question. He asked it again.

'Who am I?'

He felt himself expanding inward, as though an unsuspected world were opening within him. He shut his eyes, the better to experience this blossoming world. With a child's insistence he went on asking the same question.

'Who am I? Who am I? Who am I?'

Soon he lost himself in the question, and drifted deeper

into the flowering darkness within him. He grew fainter and felt a wonderful warmth envelop him. As he went deeper into the swirling darkness he noticed the most amazing changes taking place within him. A world was opening. He found himself emerging into an unknown world.

38

Karnak was grateful to be back in the street, relieved to have escaped the company of the money artist. He knew now for certain that artists could tell him nothing of what he sought.

As he wandered the streets, observing the faces, listening to the noises, he thought about Amalantis and wondered what he could do to find her. He still felt the question-askers might know.

He had gone past a shop when a few steps later he realised that it was a bookshop. For many decades now bookshops had been vanishing from contemporary life. This must be one of the last left. People had stopped reading books. With the changing myths, reading had begun to be perceived as a suspicious activity. Those who wanted to know more than others were thought of as pariahs. The modern idea was to be more ignorant than your neighbour. To be less well read than your neighbour was thought the greatest politeness. To say, in conversation, 'Does such a book exist?' was the height of good manners. To read books was considered dangerous. This was largely aided by the myth of the garden.

The myth, as interpreted by the state philosophers, declared that everyone was already educated. Everyone already had in them from birth all they needed to know. Education was a bringing out, not a putting in. Ignorance was therefore the higher state. The true self was supposed to emerge with education. People were not meant to fill their heads with facts, but only to re-learn what they already knew. And what they already knew was that the state was good and everything they did was leading them back to the garden of origins.

Gradually people stopped reading. Even the machines invented to make reading easier and portable fell into disuse. These machines were smaller than a coin and could hold vast libraries of books. People simply stopped reading the ancient classics. Then they couldn't read anything that required a little thought. Then they couldn't read anything but the simplest books. Then all they read were newspapers of the popular variety. Literacy vanished from the world, along with bookshops.

It was therefore with amazement that Karnak came upon the only bookshop left in the world just when he was wondering how to find the question-askers.

He took this for a sign, and went in.

39

To his surprise there were no books in the bookshop. There were only holograms of books. When he looked at one of the holograms he noticed that it was of the pages of a book being turned. Every hologram was of a different book, whose pages were being turned. Then he heard a distant voice reading out words from a book, a soothing female voice. The book was about a girl who had fallen down a rabbit-hole. He didn't know what a rabbit-hole was. Such things had disappeared ages ago.

Karnak had heard about bookshops and had been shown books when he was growing up, but he had been shown them in great secrecy. He had been given to understand that this was something people used to have, when ideas were important, but which it was now quite dangerous to have. No one was taught with books. Children were taught through information piped into their brains, through thought-pods.

He had heard about those who read. The strange ones. They read in secret. They met, like a secret society, and if they were caught terrible things happened to them. Someone in his family had disappeared that way. An uncle. Now that he thought about it Amalantis, before she disappeared, had been saying something he didn't want to hear. Something about the old books.

Karnak soon realised that the shop wasn't really a bookshop. It was a holographic museum of the lost art of books. He marvelled at the beauty of what he saw. He gazed with admiration at the pages and the printed word.

But someone was watching him from a dark corner of the room.

40

Seated at a table in a corner of the shop was a girl. She was staring at him coolly. Her presence made him jump.

She stared at him candidly. There was no evasion or shiftiness in her eyes. The directness of her gaze was something he hadn't encountered for a long time.

The way she looked at him made him feel his reality more intensely. He felt his heart beating. He felt a pulse in his neck. He felt his bones and his skin. Normally when people looked at him they made him feel that he wasn't quite there. They made him feel blurred. This young woman made him feel clear and real.

There was something else unusual about her. Something he hadn't seen for years. It eluded him. She continued to gaze at him in silence, with such steadiness that he found himself speaking even when he knew he didn't have to.

'What happened to books?'

'What do you mean by "what happened to books?"' was the girl's careful reply.

'I mean—' and here Karnak stammered, 'I mean these images make me nostalgic for books, though they disappeared long ago. What happened? Why did they disappear? I have always wanted to ask that question.'

The girl did something unexpected. She laughed. Admittedly, it was brief but it astounded him. He looked around, expecting something to happen. He wasn't sure what. Nothing did.

'The only thing that happened to books,' the girl said, 'is that people stopped reading.'

'How did we stop reading?'

'There are many views on this,' she said, with the air of one bursting with abundant research into the forbidden. 'Some historians of culture say the art of reading was outstripped by technology. We perfected machines that did our reading for us. We could have books in smaller and smaller machines anywhere. Then we simply had books piped into our brains. Then we had our books condensed into a pill. The pill could be named "The Odyssey", for example. You swallowed it and you had the book in you. We sought easier and easier ways of reading. We wanted reading to be entirely devoid of effort. As we succeeded in eliminating effort in most parts of life, books followed this trend.'

'You mean we lost the art of reading because we wanted no effort in our lives?'

'Something like that. It began with a cultural revolution in the last century. Everyone wanted an easy life. Then there were protests against elitism in art and difficulty in writing. This was really popular. The people were used to simple newspapers and publishers found that simple books sold better. Then writers simplified their language. It became the fashion to write with words no longer than two or three syllables. It was the era of short words.'

She looked at him, smiling faintly.

'Then technology made it worse. It became a kind of a revolution. Soon books became so simple that the greatest novels of the time could be read by a child of four. This was the new ideal in literature. This was the golden age of simplicity.'

She paused and flipped a switch and the holograms changed their images. A rapid succession of books flickered in the air.

'Afterwards people stopped reading because they didn't need to. Libraries had already gone anyway in the previous century. Then publishers stopped publishing. Some of them manufactured paper bags used in the great shopping arcades. Some published postcards and merchandise.'

She paused again and Karnak still tried to place the element in her that eluded him.

'But what really killed books was the great campaign against originality. The age of equality. Then we arrived at the point where, as you know, it's an insult to be better informed than your neighbour.'

She gave a short laugh.

'In our age, ignorance is genius. Sorry for such a long answer. It is not often that someone asks that question.'

'Really?'

'Yes.'

She looked at him. There was a smile in her voice when she said:

'You're our first visitor in three months.'

'Why do you have this shop then? Why an exhibition about the death of books?'

'Because of my father.'

'Who was your father? He sounds interesting.'

'He was fascinated by reading. It's a quaint notion. Someone sitting down and reading words along a line. Turning pages of a book. Isn't it odd to think of leaves of a book with words printed on both sides? Words printed with a sense of order. Words that are silent on the page and give no indication of what they sound like or what they represent. It's magic. We've tried to recreate this strange art, with the help of the few writers left…'

'There are writers left in the world!'

Suddenly the girl leapt from behind the desk and ran to the door. She stuck her head outside and looked both ways. She came back in, shut the door, and bolted it.

'You have made me say more than I should,' she said, looking worried. 'Why are you asking these questions? Who are you? What do you want?'

The change in her manner alarmed Karnak. The girl had turned fierce. He felt in danger and soon realised why. Looking very determined, and very skilled, she was holding a knife to his heart.

41

Mirababa had been climbing a ladder in the darkness of his mind. He had been climbing for a long time. The stars were clearer than he had ever seen them. Soon the ladder vanished.

He emerged in a strange world. It was a garden. There were children's voices in the wind among the trees, but he couldn't see them. An abundance of flowers met his eyes, lilies and roses and asphodels. Near the fountain there was a circle of lotuses. In the garden there were many stately trees and many beautiful birds.

He followed the voices of the children till they vanished. In their place came a tinkling melody. The fragrance of honeysuckle filled the air, and then it was gone. The beautiful things were so fleeting. He followed the lightly sounding music of a flute and it led him deep into a row of tall beeches, and into a bank of yellow roses.

Beyond the roses there was the river. It glimmered in the mysterious sunlight of that realm. It was only when he saw the river that he noticed the special quality of the light. It seemed to shine from all things.

The river sparkled. The boy sat on the riverbank and wept with happiness.

Karnak remembered how much she loved children. She used to sit on a bench in the park and watch children play. She liked watching little girls as they made up new games for themselves. Children loved her too and were always confiding to her about their friends that no one else could see. Amalantis had wanted to be a teacher, but she refused to teach because she said that everything they were made to teach was designed to kill the souls of children, designed to render them stupid before they had begun to live.

'It's a shame that loving children as you do you don't teach,' Karnak said to her one day.

'In our world,' she said, 'teaching does all the damage. I would like to unteach.'

'Unteach?'

'That is when you undo the damage that the system has done.'

'You could get into trouble talking like that.'

'We are all in trouble. It's just that we don't know it.'

Every time she said something like that an object always fell in the room. If they were out and she said something like that, he would hear a sudden loud bang near them. For a long time he thought it was just coincidence.

42

Karnak allowed the girl to lead him into a dark room. The knife had left his heart and was now thrust into his ribcage. She commanded him to sit on a chair in the pitch blackness of the room. Out of the blackness she spoke.

'Who did you say you were?'

'No one.'

'What's your name?'

'Karnak.'

'What do you want here?'

'I thought it was a bookshop.'

'So?'

'I came seeking writers.'

'Why? No one's interested in books any more. Come to think of it, no one's interested in writers any more. Except spies. Are you a spy?'

'I'm not a spy. I'm only looking for clues.'

'Clues to what?'

'Clues that I think writers can give.'

'You have too much faith in writers.'

'Why do you say that?'

'They had no great wisdom or knowledge. They should have done, but they didn't.'

'Really? Surely they knew something.'

'In the very distant past they did. Afterwards all they knew was how to write.'

'Aren't you being unfair?'

'They were part of the reason that reading declined.'

'How?'

'They lost their truth. They wrote for fame, for money. They did whatever it took to succeed in the changing times. They lost their integrity. They diluted the language of the race.'

'How did they do that?'

'They championed a downward trend and eliminated mystery from the world. They didn't trust in beauty any more. Every word became only what the word meant. A tree was a tree, nothing more. Poetry died. People couldn't think symbolically. They turned against myth. Realism became the only truth. The written word became poorer than conversation. It was no longer necessary to read because books no longer nourished, they only informed. But technology could do that more easily.'

'How do you know all this?'

'I researched it.'

'Why?'

'I'm asking the questions. What clues are you looking for?'

'I don't know, but I need help.'

'And you think writers can help?'

'I hope so. I've tried artists. But they're interested in other things.'

'You'll be disappointed.'

'Let me take the risk.'

The girl had lowered the knife. She looked at him for a long time.

'Okay. Wait here.' She spoke in a new voice.

With the faint sound of a sliding door, she was gone.

43

It was a happiness that could not last long.

Three shadows drifted over the river. Mirababa watched their approach with dread. They were the shadows of something strange and they were coming towards the garden. Alarmed, he opened his mouth and began to scream but didn't. They were just shadows drifting across the water.

For a moment the birds were quiet. The children's voices among the flowers became cries of distress. Then they were silent.

Mirababa saw the shadows drift towards him. They were the shadows of giants. Two of the shadows drifted past him, spreading darkness.

The last of them was a colossus. It came and sat beside him on the banks of the river. Its feet reached to the depths of the river and its head was just below the sky. It lowered its head and looked at Mirababa. Its eyes were bigger than the boy. They were like two large moons.

'Who are you?' Mirababa asked.

The colossus laughed. Its laughter shook the earth and sent high waves rolling on the face of the lake.

'You ask the right question at last,' the colossus boomed.

44

Karnak sat in silence in the dark room for a long time. He heard nothing and could see nothing. He wondered how long he should wait. He was beginning to think of getting up when he heard the faint sound of the door sliding open. Then a warm touch on his hand led him out of the darkness.

He entered a dazzling room. There was a bank of candles at an altar, flowers in a silver goblet, and a sword on the wall. He glimpsed a word on the ceiling, written in an elliptical script. He didn't know what the word was, but it awoke in him a feeling of expansion.

When his eyes grew accustomed to the light, he saw three skeletal figures hunched over desks. They had quills in their hands which they dipped into inkwells of gold. Their eyes were hollow and their fingers long and thin. One of them, he noticed with surprise, was a woman.

They scratched away on what may have been papyrus, dipping their quills regularly into the ink, working rapidly without pause and without stopping to think. They did not notice anything around them. They were mantled in flowing blue robes, not in any way identical, but uniform in the serious air they imparted. With thin wisps of hair, their skin unhealthy and pallid, they worked at their desks in complete silence, scratching away at the papyrus, never looking up and never pausing. It was as if the scratching away and the dipping were the sole function and meaning of their lives.

Karnak moved towards them, but the girl motioned him to stop. She led him to an adjacent room.

'What are they doing?'

'They're writing.'

'What are they writing?'

'They're writing about everything. They're the recorders. Everything that happens finds its way onto the page. They record every dream, every death, every disappearance, every laughter. Nothing escapes them. They capture every footstep, every door that opens, every leaf that falls, every scream uttered, every story told, every joke recounted, every moment that passes, every meeting between people. They fix it all in golden ink.'

'But how can they know these things?'

'They do.'

'How long do they work like that? I never saw them pause.'

'They never pause. They write all the hours of the day and night. There are not enough hours in the day for them to write in. They write about all that happens. They write in their sleep, they write while they eat, they write through all their functions. They are chasing the impossible. They must do what they do or…'

She paused. A shadow passed across her face.

'But we've got machines that do that. We've had them for hundreds of years. Every single moment of our lives is recorded in one form or other, isn't it? Why do they have to do it?'

She looked at him with compassion.

'They're the last writers left,' she said. 'Their tribe has almost entirely perished. They write with all the passion of their lost tribe. They capture what technology cannot see, record what technology cannot feel. They are the last dreamers. Since writers vanished we've only known how to exist. But we've forgotten what living is for. Our myths have been changed – we don't know our origins any more. We've lost our past. It was in our myths. So was our future. Do you sleep well at night?'

'No.'

'Nobody does. Do you know why?'

'No.'

'Because sleep has become nightmare.'

'How did that happen?'

'Too many questions. Why do you ask so many questions?'

'I never used to ask questions. We were taught not to ask questions. Then one day, not long ago, I realised that what I thought was happiness was actually hell.'

'How did you realise that?'

'I can't say. I just came into your shop searching for clues, that's all.'

'Have you found any?'

The young lover looked at her.

'Who are you really?' he asked. 'What's your name?'

'Ruslana. But I'm not sure I can help you,' she said.

'Then why are you so interested in the lost art of reading?'

'Because my father was the last guardian of the tribe of writers.'

'What happened to him?'

'He worked for the Hierarchy, in order to raise me. It was against his conscience, of course, but times were hard. He had no choice. Then he learnt things which were terrible. He began telling stories that he shouldn't have told and he talked to people he shouldn't have spoken to and he began to babble things in his sleep that he shouldn't have babbled. Then one morning, at the height of his success as the guardian of the word, there was a knock on the door. I haven't seen him since.'

'You're very brave,' he said.

'No, I'm not. I'm just continuing my father's work. It's doomed work. You're talking to a dead person. Every day I expect a knock at the door. Today the knock brought you. Tomorrow, I may be dancing with my father in the great darkness. Who knows?'

45

The colossus lifted Mirababa onto his shoulder and with great strides took him round the world. His head floated among the clouds. From that great height, he saw towns and villages, hills and highways, pyramids and temples, mountains and deserts, farms and factories, slums and office blocks. He saw wars being fought and cities being devastated. He saw countries with great walls surrounding them. He saw continents and oceans and landlocked nations. He saw cities made up only of high-rise buildings. He saw the receding forests and the narrowing rivers. He heard cries everywhere and he didn't know what the cries were about. He heard people wailing in their sleep all over the earth and he did not know why they were wailing.

At the edge of the world he saw nothing but horizon. The earth was bounded by light in the day, and by darkness at night. The earth was alone in its space. The earth rested on air, on nothing. He saw the stars and the moon and the galaxies. Beyond them he saw only horizons. He noticed that there was always more to be seen.

'Is it possible to see beyond the limits, beyond the furthest stars?' he asked the colossus.

Gentle tremors shook the earth. The colossus was laughing.

'My realm is the earth. You need someone else to take you beyond the stars,' said the colossus, amused by the simplicity of the request.

46

'I think it's time for you to go now,' Ruslana said.

'Why?'

'Your quest is not here. Besides, if you stay here too long you might get into trouble without finding what it is you seek.'

Karnak was reluctant to leave.

'But can't I…'

'You have to leave now. I've got my own work to do. Every minute brings danger nearer.'

Still he didn't move.

'You really have to go now.'

When he didn't move, Ruslana pushed him towards the door.

'Can I come and see you again when I discover something?'

'What for?' she said, shutting the door in his face. He heard the lock turn twice and then the shutters came down.

Karnak stood outside the shop for a long time, at a loss. Where was there for him to go? The artists hadn't been helpful, and the last remaining writers were engaged in tasks of monumental futility. Pondering what he had learnt so far, he wandered the endless streets. The sun was going down behind the houses.

He walked for a long time, unaware of what he was seeing, lost in his thoughts. Then he heard noises in the air. He paid them no attention. Then he heard noises in the street.

He thought someone was trying to attract his attention. But when he looked round he saw a great crowd of people gathered in a nearby square. A man in a white suit was addressing them from a platform. Karnak went closer. He asked a few people what was going on and they said the speaker was a politician. Perhaps a politician could help him with his quest?

He squeezed through a gap in the crowd till he could hear what the man was saying.

'Follow me and my party and we will fulfil the dreams of our fathers,' the politician cried, pointing his forefinger skywards. 'We will have more gardens for your children. We will destroy the dangerous people who poison our minds with words. We will eliminate the enemies of the state. Our economy is good, but we can make it better. We are protected by the Hierarchy. Our job is to make sure that no one is better than another. We must all be prosperous. Our founding fathers gave us a great myth and every day we must work harder to fulfil it. With our party in government you will sleep better at night. Those who challenge our dreams will perish in the great darkness. I call upon you to be more vigilant than ever. Enemies are among us. Spy on your neighbours. If you see anyone happier than you, report them to the authorities. If you see anyone happier than they ought to be, report them.'

The politician swept the faces of the crowd with his eyes while he spoke. He waved his hands more vigorously as his voice rose. The crowd listened to him impassively, only leaning forward slightly.

'Watch the faces of your neighbours,' he continued, after a brief pause. 'Anyone seen wandering about at night, with no clear purpose, might be a dangerous person. Report them immediately. These are good times. We have never been better. Our children are healthy, the state is strong, and there is more equality than ever. But we can be even better. There is no hunger, but there are still dangers. Our party will keep us strong. We will work hard for your good sleep…'

A sudden swell of applause drowned out the speaker. He left the platform and then another speaker came on and said generally the same things. Three other speakers mounted the platform and made almost identical speeches.

Karnak listened to it all in amazement. All the faces around him seemed to be listening intently, though he could not say for sure. Their eyes were open but they could have been asleep. There was no animation in their faces, even when they burst into loud applause.

When the last speaker finished the crowd mysteriously dematerialised. So quickly did the people leave the square that Karnak found he was virtually the only one left there. The sky darkened, and evening fell swiftly.

A little perplexed, the young lover hurried back home. He stuck to side roads, keeping his head down, so as not to be noticed.

47

As the colossus was returning to the banks of the river, Mirababa noticed something in the distance. Darkness formed and unformed in a consistent pattern round the edges of things. Beyond the dark patterns he saw glimmerings of unearthly lights. The lights trembled beyond the horizons that had no end.

'What is that blur round the edges of things?' the boy asked the colossus.

'You're not supposed to have seen that. I'm not supposed to tell you about it.'

'Why not?'

'You are not supposed to see it.'

'What is it?'

'I can't tell you.'

'Is it death?'

'It may or it may not be.'

'Has anybody seen it before?'

'Only once in a thousand years.'

'Can I get closer?'

'If you get any closer you will not be able to return.'

'What's it for?'

'If you knew that you'd know everything.

'Is it powerful?'

'More powerful than fate.'

'Who guards it?'

'No one guards it.'

'Who put it there?'

'No one put it there.'

'Is it the edge of the world?'

'No.'

'Can you see it?'

'No.'

'How do you know what I am talking about then?'

'I know you better than you know yourself.'

The boy gazed at the dark blur around the edges of the world. They filled him with awe.

'Are they demons?'

'No.'

'Are they the old gods?'

'No.'

'Is it the beginning of the abyss?'

'Why do you ask?'

'I heard that was just outside the great wall of the world.'

'No, it isn't that.'

'Then I know what it is,' said the boy, with a sunken voice.

The colossus said nothing. With great strides he returned Mirababa to the beautiful garden by the banks of the river. Then without a word he left. He became a vast shadow retreating over the waters. The boy saw the three shadows drifting away together.

He no longer felt at ease by the river, in the garden. He went back the way he had come. He went past the lilies and the roses and the fragrance of honeysuckle. He listened to the voices of children among the flowers. He feared for them.

With a heavy heart he climbed back down the never-ending ladder. He went down past the stars and found himself again in the forest, by the lake. The moon was still in the middle of the lake.

He was not the boy that he had been. He had seen something that had changed his life forever. He had seen something he should not have seen.

BOOK TWO

1

The three old bards came for Mirababa in the depths of the long night. They found him broken in spirit. The light in his eyes was dull. He was weak in body, unable to stand. They paid no attention to his condition and asked no questions about what he had experienced.

The initiation of a new myth-maker was the most sacred duty the bards had to perform. It often resulted in the death of the initiate. The boy was only broken in spirit. His death would have been more fitting.

They bore his limp form to the shrine-house at the top of the ancient mountain. The ancestors had come from the mountain with the first prophecies and the first myths inscribed on the brightness of their faces.

The boy was borne to the temple on the crest of the mountain. This was also the highest mountain remaining after the ancient lands sank beneath the oceans. Only this peak remained. There were seven levels to climb before the boy could be taken to the temple.

In the temple there was a stone slab. When the stone slab was moved aside a stone ladder was revealed which led deep down into the bowels of the pyramid-shaped mountain. In the bowels of the mountain, in a subterranean crypt, there was a room. In the middle of the rough room, lit by a single lamp, there was a sarcophagus. Mirababa was placed in the sarcophagus. He stared at them blankly as they laid him in the stone sarcophagus.

He didn't speak as they covered the sarcophagus with a heavy stone. It was like he had died before his death. The stone plunged him into darkness. He heard them leave. He heard the stone slab being dragged back into place. Mirababa was alone in the bowels of the mountain, in a stone coffin.

2

A few days later Karnak went back to the bookshop. He was haunted by the feeling that the girl knew more than she had said. When he got there he found that the shop had vanished. In its place was a florist that specialised in flowers for graves.

Karnak went in and found the place full of vases on tables and on the floor. He saw fuchsias in earthenware jars and black roses in blue urns. A big woman with a huge face sat at a table with a yellow mug of tea before her. She stared at him with hostile eyes.

'Where's the bookshop that used to be here?' Karnak asked.

'I don't know about such things. I sell flowers, that's all. Flowers for graves. Have you any dead ones you want flowers for?'

He looked round the shop. There were pink geraniums and violet roses, ochre lilies and aquamarine orchids, in rich profusion everywhere. There were yellow flowers in little pots all along the shelves. The shelves looked solid and betrayed no sign of hasty construction. The heavy fragrance of flowers made him drowsy.

He sensed at once that he wasn't going to get any information from the formidable-looking woman. He decided he would buy a pot of flowers and get answers from her indirectly.

'Can I buy a pot?'

'You can buy all of them if you want. They're flowers for the dead, and the dead will thank you for them. Which ones do you want?'

'I'm not sure.'

'I'll choose for you.'

The woman got up and waddled over to a shelf. She picked out a small pot of violet roses. When she handed the pot to him, she said:

'I wouldn't go around asking questions if I were you.'

'Why not?'

'Could get you into trouble.'

'How long has the shop been here?'

'The flower shop has been here since the beginning of time. You can have the flowers for free. Just don't come back.'

She gently edged him to the door. He went back into the street holding the flowerpot. He walked around the area in circles till he was dizzy. He found a bench below some beech trees and sat down, putting the flowerpot next to him, not knowing what to think. His thoughts still went round in circles.

After a while he became aware that children were playing football not far from him. He watched them absent-mindedly. One of the boys kicked the ball, missed the goal, and the ball rolled towards Karnak. The boy ran over to collect it. He looked at Karnak for a moment longer than necessary.

'You look like a picture sitting on that bench with your flowerpot,' the boy said.

'Do I?'

'Yes.'

'What kind of a picture?'

'A sad picture.'

'Sad?'

'But that's good,' the boy said. 'My father says sad is good, happy is bad.'

'Why does he say that?'

'I don't normally talk to strangers. But because you're sad I don't mind talking to you.'

'That's kind of you.'

'I like sad people.'

'Why?'

'My father says there's hope for someone who's sad.'

'Why does he say that?'

'I don't know. He's strange, I guess.'

'Yes, maybe.'

The other children called out to him. He waved at them.

'All the happy people we used to know have disappeared.'

'Where have they gone?'

'I don't know. The sad people are still here. Maybe that's why sad is good.'

'You're a funny child.'

'I don't know about funny. Anyway, I must be going. I'm holding up the game.'

The boy didn't leave immediately. Karnak noticed the pale quality of his face and the mark of sorrow on his brow and the calm light in his eyes. The boy ran back to the others. Karnak watched them at their game, struck by the joyless nature of their play. It was as if they were not really children, as if they had never known childhood. The joyless way they played depressed him a little. He thought it time to leave.

He got up to go and picked up the flowerpot. He saw that the roses had withered and died.

3

In the stone sarcophagus, Mirababa breathed steadily, trying not to move. In the darkness, he tried to remember instructions he had been given. He couldn't remember any. He could not think why he was here in the stone coffin.

He told himself to be still as the heat grew. Fear rose in him and roared in his veins. The darkness crowded him and the need to move overwhelmed him and panic welled up in him.

'They have not put me here to kill me,' he thought. 'They know what they are doing.'

Then, with alarm, he thought:

'They have put me here to kill me. They do not know what they are doing. I am the sacrifice for the death of the old bard. I am the sacrifice!'

Suddenly he remembered many things. He remembered moments from the stories his grandfather read to him. He remembered tales he had overheard.

He did not move. He thought:

'Darkness is the same within or without. I will shut my eyes. My own darkness is familiar to me.'

He shut his eyes. The darkness was the same, but at least it was his own. Then he thought:

'Reality is all the same. I was at the edge of the lake, with the moon in the middle of it. A girl came out of the lake.

I climbed a ladder. I was borne by a colossus. I saw the form that our people fear most. Maybe…'

But he didn't dare finish the thought. He thought another thought:

'Maybe I can be where I want to be. Maybe I am wherever I want to be. If I chose not to be here then I am not here.'

He decided to test this notion.

'First I must go back to the lake. I did not learn the lesson of the lake with the moon in the middle of it. What was the lesson? What was the first question I did not ask?'

As he thought these thoughts he noticed the heat lessen around him.

'Maybe I am supposed to die.'

The thought frightened him.

'That's it! I'm supposed to die. Then I must die.'

He tried to will his death, but couldn't. The willing made the coffin hotter. He felt the rough stone all about him in the tight space.

'I've got to get out of here. How can I get out of here while still being here? What is the question?'

He opened his eyes. The darkness was the same. He shut his eyes again. He kept his breathing slow. He was beginning to sweat. Sweating slowed down time.

Then, not knowing what he was doing but doing it anyway, without thinking, he rose out of himself. He wanted to return to the lake in the forest. To his amazement he found that he had risen out of the stone sarcophagus. He was outside it and inside it at the same time. He hovered above it in a moment of exhilaration and terror.

Then he fell back into himself in the dark.

4

It was a source of annoyance to the Hierarchy that the magnificent idea had failed. Most of those brought in for not screaming in their sleep were, upon examination, found to be innocent. This meant that those who were dangerous to the state because they did not wail in their sleep had somehow realised they were under surveillance. This meant that the dangerous ones were mimicking the screams of the ordinary citizens.

The problem now was how to distinguish those who were truly screaming in their sleep from those who were pretending. Many solutions were put forward. For instance, random checks were suggested. Also proposed were night raids to see if people were really in bed asleep or if they were up to criminal activity and pretending to scream to cover it up. This was rejected as too intrusive. Someone suggested a machine that could detect fake screamers. But the range of sleep-screaming was so extensive that this was judged impractical. Besides it would cost too much. They set up a subcommittee to look into unobtrusive ways of identifying those who did not seem to be what they were.

Meanwhile, arrests were stepped up. Sudden searches in public places were instituted. Devices for listening in on every activity of the citizen were mobilised.

The wailings grew louder and longer every night and began to encroach on the dawn.

5

Sometimes, in the middle of the day, someone would break down and begin screaming. It could be on a busy street or in a crowded market. A man in his car with his wife and children had burst into tears while he was driving. He had pulled in at the side of the road and wailed uncontrollably. A woman buying lingerie in a shop had suddenly doubled up and begun screaming inconsolably. These isolated acts went unnoticed at first.

But then in the middle of an important board meeting the chairman had broken down and started sobbing. At a gathering of the world's financiers one of the sages of industry had begun laughing and the laughter had turned into wailing. At a parade before military generals and commanders a celebrated hero had begun to shout and howl as if possessed. He had to be led away, amidst universal bafflement. At a school, in a classroom, a teacher began howling and jabbering. At a meeting of Heads of State one of them began screaming and wailing. Something unprecedented was going on in the world.

For a long time these outbreaks went unreported and were generally covered up. Swift explanations were given for the unexpected departure of public figures from a rostrum, or for the sudden disappearance of politicians during an election campaign.

Young girls were seen exploding in grief. Grown men in pubs, drinking contentedly a moment before, would fall into shouting and wailing. Doctors at operating tables yielded inexplicably to fits of lamentation and howling. Even pilots, in mid-flight, had to be removed from duty because an excess of unhappiness and howling had come upon them.

This new wailing plague crept upon the world, from one continent to another, till it became a universal contagion. No one knew its cause. No one could propose its cure. The newspapers were silent about it, even when the managing editors, during editorial meetings, found tears pouring down their hardened faces, for no visible reason.

He began to think of Amalantis. He found it hard to think of her. To bring her to mind was to suffer intensely.

He always used to wonder why she had chosen him. She had so many people in the world to choose from and she had chosen him. He had always felt, in some way, quite unworthy of her. One day he raised the subject, and she laughed.

She was like that. She never concealed anything about herself, but there was always something mysterious about her. He had never met anyone who had such a feeling for the suffering of people. Once they were going for a walk to her mother's place. An old man ahead of them fell down and began gasping for air. She went and sat beside him, talking to him gently. Then she laid his head on her lap, while waiting for help to arrive. The old man died in her lap, with the most peaceful smile on his face. Amalantis accompanied his body to the mortuary and came every day to talk to his body. At his funeral she was there. And for a month after his burial she still went to his grave and spoke to it, as if he were still alive.

'But why do you do that?' Karnak asked her. 'He's gone now. He doesn't need anything any more.'

'Doesn't he?' she said. 'The dead need our love as much as the living.'

When she said things like that she scared him a little.

6

At first it was assumed that the weeping contagion was caused by the dangerous ones, the terrorists of words. It was even suspected that the world's water had been poisoned. Extensive chemical tests proved nothing.

Curiously enough, during the wailing contagion no words appeared on walls. Nothing new was painted on doors, billboards or streets. No leaflets blew in the wind bearing new words designed to cause unrest. The silence of the question-askers increased the suspicion of the authorities that they were the cause of the new emotional plague.

Then, in another stroke of genius, the Hierarchy came up with a temporary solution to the atmosphere of grief pervading the world. A season of festivals was decreed.

It began with the great carnival of state.

7

Karnak noticed the change in the air one day as he went about his mission of finding the question-askers. He had been awaiting a summons from the Work Generation Centre for employment, a summons that never came.

He was at the market, buying oranges, when a vegetable seller nearby burst into tears. He wept loudly and passionately and threw himself on the ground. His carrots and spinach were scattered all about him. As he wailed he gasped for air. Not long afterwards the butcher fell to screaming and had to be restrained. The police descended on the scene and began dispersing people. Then one of the policemen, the fiercest of the lot, started weeping and howling. He wept like a grief-stricken child and was quickly hustled away.

The people around looked on with pale eyes. When the young lover looked closely at them he saw they were in a state worse than shock. They were enervated, half-asleep, exhausted. He noticed their deathly pallor, their lack of animation or interest in anything. It was as if being alive were too immense an effort.

Karnak left the market. He didn't want to get hauled in with those who were being beaten and taken away by the police. As he was hurrying away, he saw a woman with two children burst into tears. She screamed and cried pitifully. Further on down the street a beautiful young girl started weeping as if she had heard of the death of her mother. The police swiftly took her away.

He did not know where to go. Wherever he went grief and wailing burst out all around him. He went down a street and heard sudden cries from inside a jeweller's shop. He saw bank managers being bundled away by the police, wracked with sobs as they were carried into waiting vans.

As he went through one of the banking districts a middle-aged banker threw himself from a third storey window. In the same district a woman lawyer threw herself from a bridge.

That night the howling was intolerable. To prevent himself hearing it, Karnak began to wail too, at the top of his voice, with all his lungs, like a wounded animal.

8

The carnival was unleashed on the world one fine Saturday morning. Floats carrying giant laughing figures paraded down the streets. Clowns and jugglers, acrobats and stand-up comics, television personalities and musicians performed on open platforms, in parks, and on the back of moving trucks, often accompanied by a host of dancing girls.

Music pounded from loudspeakers in public squares. There were events in community centres. The parks were filled with food vendors, sweet-sellers, Chinese dragons, African masquerades, celebrated singers, and fakirs. There were parades, aerial displays, and free drinks everywhere.

Sheepishly, the populace ventured out to watch pharaohs on large floats, cowboys and Indians, and public shamans. They witnessed the Samba, the Charleston, the Foxtrot, and Russian folk dances. Their competing music crowded the air. The carnival was a source of surprise to people. They were unused to anything of that nature. It had been a long time since there had been any celebration in the cities and hamlets. They poured down the streets to watch the floats. They watched folk singers from all over the world. They saw girls costumed as giant butterflies. They saw men clothed as gods and heroes. They watched as if they were witnessing a foreign invasion.

Suspicious and pale, they took the free food and free

drinks. With red-rimmed dull eyes, they listened to the stand-up comics and celebrity singers. The gaiety of the carnival, its vigorous music, its energetic performers, filled the air with a strange hollow noise.

By evening the nature of the carnival staged by the Hierarchy had begun to change.

9

There were other things being distributed at the carnival besides the free food and drinks. Leaflets were dropping from the air. Along with the food in their hands the people found leaflets with the image of sleepwalkers. Beneath the image was the single word:

UPWAKE!

Amidst the blare of atonal music, amidst the noise of percussive distraction, a single word intoned on a piercing microphone was heard. It cut through the dissonance.

UPWAKE!

Amidst the dancing girls and the company of jugglers, among the floats with effigies of heroes, a giant banner would be unfurled. It would have a single word, in large red letters:

UPWAKE!

The police were summoned when the leaflets began to be found and they arrested many performers. People found near the leaflets were carted away. Floats with unfurling banners of the dangerous word were brutally shut down. Chaos entered the carnival.

10

Karnak wandered in a daze through the feverish dream. He thought he had strayed into the land of the dead. Then he thought that the world had gone mad.

He wandered down crowded streets full of fear. At any moment something sinister might erupt from the earth. He feared sudden acts of madness. He expected the air to burst open and reveal demons. He was increasingly nervous.

He felt alien among the rough music and the floats with their costumed dancers. He went to hear a stand-up comic and found nothing he said amusing. A famous young band performing their latest officially sanctioned music made him feel flat. The belly dancers and the jugglers gave him the absurd sense that at any minute the whole edifice would collapse and ordinary life would be left standing in its place. A sheaf of leaflets descended on him. Where had they come from?

One leaflet struck his face. He peeled it off and beheld the image of a man fast asleep, wearing a suit, crossing the street. Above the image, was the single word:

UPWAKE!

Karnak threw the leaflet away in horror and fled from the vicinity. He ran till he came to a small park. He stopped at a tree and tried to regain his breath. Carved into the trunk was a single word.

UPWAKE!

Not knowing what else to do, Karnak sank to his knees, and began to weep.

11

Who knows what turned that carnival of state into a carnival of weeping? The people walked listlessly alongside the floats. They watched the tumbling acrobats with hollow eyes. They listened to the Indian musicians and gazed upon the Chinese dragons with dulled faces. The performers were animated but found the air resistant.

Whole streets were brought to a standstill. The police were busy everywhere, trying to rid the carnival of the pamphlet-spreaders. In unexpected places, flowered the word:

UPWAKE!

From the tops of trees leaflets came cascading down. From vents in the ground a loudhailer would punctuate the air with the word:

UPWAKE!

There would be a harmless explosion in the square and one of the military statues would be draped with a flapping white banner. In red and blue letters there was one word:

UPWAKE!

A policeman climbed the statue to take down the banner, but became entangled in it. From his neck the word fluttered in the breeze. When they brought him down he seemed inexplicably traumatised. He was seen weeping as he was led away.

It wasn't long before people heard weeping from the interior of one of the Chinese dragons. The Indian dancers in the square began crying. The acrobats had tears streaming down their painted faces. A famous singer, in the full flood of his crooning, suddenly fell to sobbing. Then the contagion spread.

Floats of dancers became floats of wailers. The Brazilian Samba dancers were seen howling. The African masquerades wept as they danced. The carnival had changed.

The police looked on helplessly, not knowing who to arrest. The crowds of people, with dull eyes and pale faces, looked on without emotion. Then as if at a pre-arranged sign the crowds began to disperse. Apart from the broken performers, the streets and squares became empty.

12

The boy in the stone sarcophagus felt the darkness was alive. He felt it sliding on his skin, seeping into his bones. He felt it nibbling at his flesh, crawling on his face. Breathing was difficult in the heavy darkness.

In his thoughts he tried to return to the lake. The more he tried the more he felt his entombment. He breathed in the darkness. Parts of his body were going numb. The numbness spread. He felt himself turning to stone.

A second wave of panic hit him. He fought against the embrace of stone, and felt the hopelessness of the struggle. Then he heard a voice in the darkness of his mind.

'Go in.'

He became still. There was no more in to go. He wanted to get out. He didn't want to go in. He was in. If he went any more in he would perish.

There were voices in the dark. Were they the voices of demons? Did he have demons in the coffin with him?

'How can I escape? How can I be free?'

He asked himself the question again and again.

'How can I be free?'

He thought about the question.

'Who is the I? Who am I?'

He asked the new question over and over.

'Who am I?'

He asked himself other questions. He was full of questions now.

'If I know who I am, I will know how to be free. Who am I?'

He heard the same answer in the dark. It grew fainter and fainter, till it was less than a whisper. He heard it more clearly for being so faint.

'Go in.'

Like one who has nothing to lose, who can gamble everything on a single throw, he turned his thoughts inward, and went in.

13

Many days passed and the carnival faded from memory. Karnak still wandered the streets searching for clues. His quest became stronger. Then one day as he walked the streets he noticed something he hadn't seen before.

He had looked at people and had seen paleness of skin and dullness of eyes. Sarcasm had become permanent and cynicism had left its dryness on their features. Gloom, misery, fear, and resentment were stamped on their faces. He had seen death on the brows of children. He had seen crowds marked for death and whole families marked for disappearance. He had seen pretty girls marked for madness. There was not a single face that was not doomed in some way. He had come to accept the fact that so many were marked with despair.

He had seen them walking on bridges. Faces without faces. Seen them walk the misty streets with their faces turned backwards. Seen them with bowler hats with blood on their faces. He had seen them in three piece suits with blood in their mouths, as if they had been supping on live animals. Seen them in ball gowns with blood on their lips. He had seen them in the banks, counting money with blood on the notes, in fashion houses with blood on their hands. He had seen people with their faces cracked like masks, had seen them praying in the churches with blood dripping from the chalice, blood seeping from the bibles. He had seen priests with blood on their cassocks. Figures in mosques with blood oozing from the book of the Prophet. He had seen children with blood in their eyes. He had seen two people kissing, drawing blood from their mouths as if devouring one another.

He had seen them in pubs drinking and smoking with blood on the cigarettes. He had seen them playing football and kicking the fallen instead of the ball. He had passed people walking along the river who were shouting at themselves. Watched the audience in a theatre suddenly bawling as one. He had seen actors commit suicide on stage, during their performances. Seen a funeral cortège in which a coffin had burst open and the dead one had let out a final shout before settling back into oblivion. He had heard someone singing at night instead of screaming and a sudden bulletburst extinguishing the song.

He had seen these things and had come to accept that death and bad dreams stalked the land.

But one day he saw something he had never seen before, and it frightened him. He saw on someone's face the glimmer of a smile.

14

Mirababa went in. He went into the darkness of himself. He went deep down as far as he could go. He found nothing. Only the same darkness. He was disappointed. As he had nowhere else to go, he stayed in the disappointment. The darkness changed. He noticed its texture and softness, a whirling, changing quality. It was not darkness at all, but some kind of cloud-like substance. He was so fascinated he did not notice the substance change.

Suddenly he saw about him, not too clearly, but clearly enough, a field or a park. He saw people dancing and people watching them dance. He was among them but they didn't see him. Then he found himself by the lake. It was dark and there was no moon. He sat there for a long time.

Then he found himself somewhere else. He wasn't sure where. Towers rose high up in the air. People streamed down the streets. Their eyes faced downwards and they walked as if they were not alive. Someone in the street screamed out loud. Troubled by the scream, the boy found himself back in the cloud-like darkness of the stone sarcophagus.

15

Karnak had seen the glimmer of a smile on the face of a woman in the crowd. He saw it and then it was gone. It was some time before he realised what he had seen.

The smile frightened him at first. It seemed monstrous. Why had it frightened him? He wasn't sure.

But then he had turned around and gone looking for the face with the secret smile. He hurried back down the street, past shops and galleries. He went past the post office and the giant towers of state. He ran on ahead, past the crowds. Then he came back, walking against the flow, searching faces, seeking that elusive smile. He didn't find it.

Karnak tried many roads, back streets, crowded places, pubs, and train stations, but still could not find it. Then he tried to find anyone with a trace of the smile. They might know something that could help him.

Many days passed. He never saw anyone with the glimmer of a smile.

He wondered if he had dreamed it.

16

Karnak was sitting on a park bench one day with nothing on his mind when the little boy who had spoken to him before appeared in front of him.

'You're still sad. I like that.'

'What?'

'That you're still sad.'

'What're you doing here anyway?'

'I'm playing with my friends.'

'Shouldn't you be at school?'

'Playing is school.'

'You should be at school.'

'I don't like school.'

'Why not?'

'I don't like the stories they tell us.'

'Why not?'

'My father says the stories are all lies. I like the old ones.'

'Which old ones?'

'The ones they used to tell a long time ago.'

'What stories are those?'

'My father told me not to tell anyone.'

'Why not?'

'I don't know,' the little boy said. 'People are funny, I suppose.'

'What stories do they tell you now that you don't like?'

'Silly stories.'

'Like what?'

'Do you want me to tell you one?'

'Yes, please.'

'Okay. Are you ready?'

'Yes.'

'Once upon a time there was a little girl who did what she was told. She always did what she was told. She always believed what she was told. She grew up and married a handsome man and had beautiful children and lived happily ever after.'

'Is that it?'

'Yes. It's silly, isn't it?'

'I think so.'

'But it is, isn't it?'

'Yes, it is.'

'Do you want another one?'

'Maybe.'

'Yes or no?'

'Yes. One more.'

'Once upon a time there was a boy. He worked very hard at school and did all his homework. He liked playing in the great garden that the leaders had given us. This boy did what he was told. He was very obedient and never talked back. He studied hard and did everything he was told and grew up and married the most beautiful girl who also worked hard and did what she was told. They had lots of children and they travelled round the world and everyone liked them. They had lots of money and they lived happily ever after.'

'Is that it?'

'Yes. Isn't it silly?'

'I don't know.'

'It is.'

'Maybe it is.'

'It is. My father says so.'

'Who is your father?'

'I'm not supposed to answer that question.'

'Why not?'

The little boy gave Karnak a quizzical look, as though something was not quite right about his face.

'I like it that you're still sad. There's hope for you, my father would say. I've got to be going now.'

Then the boy was gone. He rejoined his mates at their game under the big oak tree. Karnak looked at them for a while. When a wave of melancholy swept over him, he resumed his wandering and his quest.

17

Karnak's wandering took him far into the city streets. He thought about the little boy's stories and the more he thought about them the sadder he grew. He was about to cross a road when he heard someone calling for help. He couldn't see where the voice was coming from.

'Please help. It's stuck.'

A man standing at the back of a van was waving him over.

'I need to get this wheelchair down. It's stuck,' the man said in a dry voice.

Karnak sprang forward. Together they wriggled the wheelchair out of the groove in which it was caught. Then they rolled it down into the street. In the wheelchair was an old lady. She was dressed in a gaudy fashion, in pink trousers and a red shirt, and was heavily made-up. She seemed either fast asleep or dead. The man who had asked for his help had one good eye and one bad one. He was tall and a little stooped.

'Help me get her into the hospital,' he said.

'The hospital?'

'There. Right in front of you. Don't you have eyes?'

Karnak looked up and saw a gleaming white building with stately columns, marble stairs and frosted windows. It was the hospital. He had never noticed it before.

'Don't just stare. Help me!'

In a bit of a daze, Karnak began pushing the wheelchair

towards the big double doors. Inside, the lobby was vast and semi-circular and sunlit, but it had a pervasive mood of gloom. Everything looked new. They went up in the lift to the third floor.

'Just help me get her into that ward over there and you'll have done your good deed for the day,' said the one-eyed man gruffly.

Karnak rolled the chair into the ward. What he saw astonished him.

18

In the stone sarcophagus, Mirababa felt his limbs grow numb. He was a little less afraid of the darkness now. He tried not to move. He tried to keep his breathing even. He listened, but heard nothing. Imprisoned in stone, unable to move, refusing to panic, having nowhere else to go, he turned around into himself and plunged into the thick darkness within.

Then he heard voices. One of the voices said he was going to die. Another said he was dead already. A third said he had been abandoned by the bards, sacrificed by the race. Voices laughed at his foolishness for believing he was involved in anything noble. Others laughed at all the stories he had heard and believed, all the myths he had been taught. One voice said his grandfather was a fraud. Another voice said there were no questions, no answers, no original prison, no in or out. There was just death.

'Everything is only death. Death is all there is. The rest is illusion. And life is the biggest illusion of all.'

The boy listened patiently, fascinated. He wondered what the voices were. He wondered where they came from.

'Who are you?' he asked.

'We are you.'

'You can't be me. I am me.'

'We are parts of you.'

'You can't be parts of me.'

'Why not?'

'How can you be parts of me and be saying such horrible things to me?'

'We are the horrible parts of you.'

'I don't have horrible parts.'

'Yes, you do. Everyone does.'

'You can't be part of me because I'm not an enemy to myself.'

'How do you know?'

'Because I'm not.'

'If we are not part of you, who do you think we are then?'

'I don't know.'

'We are you.'

'You're not. And if you are, either help me or shut up.'

The voices fell silent. Their silence surprised him. Then he found himself in a vast open space. It was big and round and had no definite substance. The space seemed infinite, but it wasn't. It was bounded by something. But he didn't know what it was. He rested in that space and listened.

19

Karnak saw a strange wild celebration in the hospital ward, a bacchanalia all around him. Patients just back from operations or waiting to be operated on exploded in raucous merriment. With tubes coming out of their noses and chests, they were spouting rough vulgar jokes, coughing and laughing and clowning around. Some of them were demonstrating funny walks. Some were showing off their private parts, bending over, exposing their rear ends. Many were talking feverishly in tongues.

Most of them were already drunk. They'd thrown their mattresses on the floor and were banging on the metal beds with their false legs, telling loud stories about outrageous sexual encounters from their youths.

They were all talking at once, raising their voices, shouting each other down, laughing at nothing.

The ones who were too ill to move, bandaged like mummies, or paralysed by strokes, laughed with their eyes, or tapped away with their fingers and feet. They made loud insistent groans that were grotesque forms of laughter.

Karnak was shocked by the mood in the ward. These were the dying, the terminally sick, advanced cancer patients, and they were happy. He had never seen such merriment, never heard such laughter, such free expression of feelings and language.

He heard an old man cursing the system. He heard dying women singing bawdy songs, screaming and laughing. One of the old women with a fine face and rheumy eyes turned to him and said:

'I wish I had lived the life I really wanted to live. This is my last chance!'

Then she laughed and took her clothes off and pounced on an old man on the bed next to her. Karnak didn't have a moment to be outraged or amazed before someone shouted something behind him that made him turn around. He saw a woman with a bandaged face. She was elaborating a rude joke about the Hierarchy. In a far corner of the ward a man, bound to the bed, was singing a bawdy version of the national anthem, interspersed with burps and lower wind noises and harsh joyful laughter. Right next to Karnak, a little old woman, trampling on her bed, was incanting in a cracked voice fragments of the myth of the original prison. She was reciting as if it were a mantra against death.

All about him was an orgy of coughing and spluttering, fornicating and laughing. For a moment he thought that the proximity of death had unhinged them all. Then he saw something he really didn't expect.

The old lady he had helped carry into the hospital had woken up from her sleep. Surrounded by all the noise and uproar, she had perked up. Though she was bound to her wheelchair, she was bouncing up and down, waving her arms, her face animated.

'Yes, you're right. I never lived before,' she cried. 'I never lived. Frightened of everything all my life. Frightened of death. Why did I ever give a fuck? I want my life back! Give me back my life, you bastards. You bastards filled me with fear and I never lived a single moment of my life. I want my life back, you bastards…'

Then she began leering and twisting in her chair. She was flushed with happiness like a girl at her first party.

Karnak turned to the one-eyed man.

'I don't understand. What's going on?'

'Nobody understands,' the one-eyed man said. 'But, if you ask me, they seem like the happiest people in the land. And they are all about to die.'

'You mean they're happy to be dying?'

'They're having a ball, and no one can stop them. The authorities have tried sedating them, but they just keep on laughing and telling jokes and cursing till one by one they drop dead.'

Karnak looked about him. A man strapped to a nearby bed was singing a revolutionary song in a stentorian voice. Over by the window, a woman was singing loudly about the best sex she ever had. All the other women joined in her laughter.

It was as if they were drunk on death. Sticking two fingers up at life. Then he noticed something else. They were throwing leaflets at one another and had even plastered sections of the walls with them. Lower down the walls were sprayed with the dangerous word:

UPWAKE!

On a far wall he saw the words:

WHO IS THE PRISONER?

On the back of a door there was scrawled:

QUESTION!

In bold yellow letters in the middle of a wall he saw:

ESCAPE!

On the floor near his feet, he read:

LIES!

He looked up and on the ceiling saw one word:

HELL.

Across two beds was draped a banner, which read:

THE UNEXAMINED LIFE…

All along the floor, written, it seemed, in blood, were the words:

UPWAKE, SLEEPERS!

Scribbled across the heads of four beds was the legend:

IN THE BEGINNING WAS THE PRISON…

Assaulted by all these signs and by the laughter and noise and cursing pouring at him from all corners of the ward, the young lover felt dizzy. An onrush of vertigo overcame him. The world seemed to have tilted upside down. He backed out of the ward and fled through the hospital corridors as if a horde of mad men were after him. He ran out screaming into the streets.

One day they had an argument. It lasted all day. She didn't raise her voice the whole time. They argued about the idea of books. She thought they should be brought back.

'But why? If they disappeared there must have been a good reason for their disappearance.'

'Is that true of people too?'

'What people? I don't know what you're talking about.'

'I know. But sometimes things disappear because they are made to disappear.'

'But why would anybody do that?'

'Because the world is not what you think.'

'You keep saying that. But you don't have any proof.'

'I don't have any proof because things are done so invisibly.'

'How do you know for sure then if they're done so invisibly?'

'You mustn't always wait for proof before you know something is wrong. By the time you get proof, it might be too late.'

'What are you to believe then, if not proof?'

'The absences, the silences, the number of those who go mad…'

'You can't measure a world by absences, can you?'

'Absences are the most revealing things.'

'But surely an absence is an absence. It can't reveal anything.'

'Only absences can reveal.'

'You have strange ideas.'

'It's a wonder you don't worry more about absences.'

'What do you mean?'

'The disappearance of your parents, for example.'

'Let's leave my parents out of it.'

'Why?'

'There must have been a good reason why they vanished.'

'That's what they tell us.'

'And I believe them. Otherwise I would go mad.'

'That might be better for you.'

'Anyway, how can silence be revealing?' he said, trying to change the subject. 'Silence is silence.'

'Silence is not silence. Some silences scream.'

'How do you know all these things?'

'I don't know. I just know them. I've always known them.'

'Then why are you with me, who doesn't seem to know these things?'

'But you do.'

'Do I? How can you say that?'

'You'll see.'

'I wonder how you can love me. You make me feel so…'

'So what?'

'So asleep.'

'You're not asleep. You're just grieving.'

'Grieving? For what?'

'For everything.'

'Nonsense.'

'You'll see.'

'Do you love me?'

'Yes.'

'As I am?'

'As you are, as you were, and as you will be.'

'Sometimes you make me feel so inadequate.'

'We're all inadequate. And we're not. You're special.'

'Me? I don't feel it. It's only your love makes me special.'

They argued all day and not once did she raise her voice. When she was most annoyed she sounded most gentle. Sometimes this irritated and puzzled him. She rarely argued, though, and this day she really argued. She would not let any points go. Her quiet persistence wore him out. She tracked down every minor inconsistency. She questioned his assumptions. She kept probing at something in him. She did it with a tiny flower of a smile in her eyes. He didn't get what she was aiming at.

'You don't normally argue. Why are you arguing so much today?'

'What's wrong with a good argument?'

'It shows real discord. It makes me feel we're so different. It frightens me a little.'

'I don't know. I think only those who truly love can truly argue. It means I feel safe with you to express my truest thoughts. Who else am I going to do it with?'

'But it can't be good to argue.'

'Not if you argue all the time.'

'I hate arguments. I was taught never to argue.'

'But if you never argue you never really know the other person. You never really know yourself.'

'I always think that when you argue it means you don't love.'

Amalantis looked at him steadily, with that smile of hers that he could never understand.

'It's only because I love you that I argue with you.'

Then they made love. They made love slowly and passionately and longingly. Their lovemaking was the other side of their argument, its dance and celebration. They made love the way they had never made love before, with new discoveries and new cries. They made love until they both shone in an unholy, carnal light.

20

In that vast space, Mirababa noticed a girl sitting next to him. It was the same girl that had emerged from the moon-lit lake. She sat silently, a smile on her face. It was a beautiful smile and it filled the space with an unusual light.

'Why are you smiling?'

'Why are you not smiling?'

'Why should I smile?'

'Because you're dead.'

'Am I dead?'

'Yes.'

'How do you know?'

'Because you're here.'

'Where is here?'

'The place where the dead go first.'

'It's a nice place.'

'Do you want to stay?'

'No.'

'Why not?'

'The time isn't right.'

'What do you want to do?'

'I want to know things.'

'What do you want to know?'

'Is the original myth true?'

'What myth?'

'That we are born into prison.'

'Yes.'

'Why?'

'Why what?'

'Why are we born into prison?'

'Because that is what birth is.'

'Why is that?'

'Because that which is great is born into that which is small. That which is infinite is born into that which is finite.'

'Can you ever get out of the prison?'

'You're out of it now.'

'I mean, when you're alive, can you get out of the prison?'

'Yes. Rarely.'

'What do you have to do?'

'You must realise what you are. The sea must find its source. The great in you must find the great that it comes from.'

'How can you do that?'

'You can do it in a moment or in ten thousand years.'

'Why is it so rare?'

'Because people believe what is small in them rather than what is great.'

The girl had been smiling, but now her smile was luminous.

'Why are you smiling like that?'

'Because you have to make a choice.'

'What choice?'

'Whether to wake up or remain asleep.'
'I thought you said I was dead?'
'You won't be dead forever.'

21

The further he was from the hospital where the dying were happy, the easier Karnak breathed. The experience troubled him. The living are miserable but the dying are happy, was the first clear thought he'd had in a long time.

He wandered aimlessly, trying to walk out his distress. He let his feet lead him where they wanted. They led him, after a long while, to the flower-seller's shop. The bell above the door rang as he went in. He saw the bad-tempered woman sitting behind a table as if she hadn't moved since the last time he had seen her.

'You sold me flowers that died as soon as I left here,' he said.

'That's not my fault,' she replied grumpily.

Karnak stared at her. Without thinking, without wanting to, he snatched up a knife from the table and pounced on her. He pinned her against the wall and held the knife at her neck.

'Where did the girl go?' he shouted in her ear. 'The girl in the bookshop. What happened to the bookshop? What did you do to her? How did you get here? Who are you? Answer my questions or by the name of hell I will stab you to death here and now!'

The woman, startled by his sudden fury, saw madness in his eyes, his hand poised to thrust the knife into her.

'Don't kill me,' she said quietly. 'I'll tell you. Just don't hurt me.'

'Speak!' he yelled. 'Speak! I've had enough! Speak, or your blood will be spattered over these flowers!'

'I'll speak,' she cried. 'Just take the knife off my neck. Please.'

He didn't know how the knife had come to be in his hand. He relaxed his grip on her, but not the tension of the knife.

She began to speak.

22

Mirababa noticed that he was alone again in the vast space. The girl had gone, but something of her smile remained.

Sitting there in the darkness he conceived a sudden desire to see the stars. Before he knew it, he was soaring through the interstellar realms at an alarming speed. The stars were like flowers in a garden. There seemed no end to them, to scattered jewels of stars, clusters and constellations. He shot through galaxies where stars were like frozen fireworks in the shining darkness. Deep in space, in a celestial blackness, he heard a voice say:

'What're you doing here?'

'I came to see the stars.'

'What do you want?'

'I want freedom.'

'Freedom from what?'

'Freedom from death.'

After an interstellar silence, the deep voice said:

'Come, follow me.'

Mirababa felt himself taken by the hand. Then he was hurtling at great speed into a storm of whiteness. He saw the turning worlds. He saw the ten thousand things. He saw the great book of destiny. In a flash he read the past, present, and future of all things.

'Use well what you have seen,' said the voice.

Before he knew it, he was back in the stone sarcophagus, in a state of bliss that bordered on madness.

23

The flower-shop woman said:

'I am one of those people that the Hierarchy moves into houses taken over from trouble-makers. Some of us are carpenters. We only use wood supplied by the state. Some of us are butchers, but we only sell meat provided by the state. I sell flowers provided by the state. I'm not really a flower-seller.'

'What are you then?'

'I work with the dead. Now I sell flowers meant only for the dead.'

'How does that work?'

'The flowers aren't meant to last long. The dead don't need them.'

'How did you get to be here?'

'I was given orders to move here. On the day I came the police had just been in and destroyed all the furniture.'

'What about the girl?'

'What girl?'

'The girl who used to run the bookshop?'

'I don't know anything about the bookshop. But I did see a girl that day. She was watching the shop from across the road. I think she had something to do with the place.'

'Why do you think that?'

'By the way she looked.'

'How did she look?'

'Like she was leaving her life behind.'

'And what about the bookshop?'

'There wasn't much left when the police came in. They found this strange machine, but no books.'

'Manuscripts?'

'No manuscripts.'

'Printing presses? Paper?'

'No printing presses, no paper. They found no one.'

'No one?'

'No one. Just the tables, shelves, ink pots, chairs, and the machine. They destroyed it all. I moved in the same day. A van brought furniture and flowers to last a week. The walls were repainted and they put up a new sign.'

'What happened to the girl?'

'Ask those dangerous people.'

'Who?'

'You know, the ones who are always putting up those words everywhere. When the police had gone I saw the girl across the road and I went outside to see what she was up to. Then I found these plastered on my door.'

'What?'

She pulled open a drawer and took out two leaflets. Each one had the same design, a red rose, a star, and the legend:

SLEEPER, UPWAKE!

'I didn't see her again.'

Karnak dropped the knife on the table. He stood in thought

for a long time. He was about to leave when the flower-shop woman said:

'There was something strange about her.'

'What?'

'Something I'll never forget.'

'What was it?'

'Her smile.'

24

Mirababa fell asleep in the stone coffin. He slept for a long time, the sleep of oblivion. When he woke, he had no idea what he was doing there in that tight space. He had no idea what he was doing in that darkness. He tried to remember and the thought occurred to him that a terrible mistake had been made and he had been buried alive. He was beginning to panic when he heard a distant sound. Then he thought he had imagined it. He listened intently. There was only silence.

He waited and was still. Then after a while he heard the noise again. Something was being dragged, stone across stone. He heard footsteps. Then more silence. Then he heard voices. He remained still. Somehow he knew he must not be overcome by hope. He breathed evenly, and kept his eyes shut. Then it went silent. Should he scream? What if he had imagined the sounds? What if he screamed himself into terror? But if he didn't scream they might not know he was there. He kept very still, breathing evenly. He kept still for a long time. Then he must have blanked out, for when he came to he heard them dragging away the stone cover. He felt the air on his face. A voice above him said:

'Is he still alive?'

'Raise him up with the master's grip, and see.'

Mirababa felt a strange grip on his hand and forearm and shoulder. He felt himself being lifted into the air.

25

Karnak knew now what he must do. His quest had been simplified. He must find Ruslana, the girl of the books.

He had left the flower-seller's shop and walked round the neighbourhood. The rows of neat houses had bright façades, but there was something heavy and dark and sad-looking about them. Even the trees planted at regular intervals seemed to protest against being there. Their leaves, green and grey, added nothing lively to the streets. He walked around half-expecting to see something. He didn't know what.

He looked differently at people's faces now. Before he had looked without seeing. Maybe even looked without wanting to see. Now he was looking for a face with a smile or the reflection of a smile.

Many days passed like that. He wandered, he searched, he looked at faces. His wandering proved pointless, his search fruitless, and he saw nothing special in the faces, only anxiety and the fear that had always been there.

After many days he returned to the neighbourhood of the flower-seller. He hoped that Ruslana would also be drawn back to her past. He stood a good distance away, concealed behind one of the limp trees that didn't want to be there, and watched the flower-seller's shop. He never saw anyone go in. No one ever bought flowers there. For a while he could not believe it. But after many hours, and many days, he realised that it was so.

At first this was merely a strange fact. But while walking one day, in an adjacent neighbourhood, he saw another flower-seller's shop. It was identical to the first one. He stopped and watched it for hours. No one went in there either. No one bought flowers.

26

As the weeping plague spread, clinics were opened to cope with the volume of the contagion. The wailing at night had extended into the daytime. First the dawns were punctuated with sudden cries, as of someone being murdered. The police would investigate and would find that it was a woman wailing as she prepared to go to work; or a man in the bath, screaming as if his entrails were being torn out of him. Then it became more common.

On the buses, on the trains, in the underground, a man would crease up into tears. People looking at him would soon start weeping too. A lady with severe lipstick would dissolve into sobs. The people who tried to comfort her would themselves succumb to sobbing.

It became common also for people to start wailing in the offices, as if overcome by an unaccountable access of grief. The doctors never found any history of madness in these people, or melancholy, or depression. There was no history of crisis or loss in their families. They were all normal citizens.

The weeping plague swept across the globe, leaping across oceans, descending on isolated villages, and wrecking famous cities. It became a universal hazard. Accidents proliferated around the world, in factories, building sites, on the highways, in nuclear power stations. A new kind of doctor emerged, just for the treatment of this new condition. But the Hierarchy denied the existence of the plague. Not a single mention was made of it in the media.

27

Through all this the media was preoccupied with news of the rich and famous. It seemed they were the only ones who existed. The front pages of the newspapers were crowded with pictures of the latest celebrities. Mines collapsed in remote mountainous regions, with hundreds of men trapped below, but the newspapers chronicled the love lives of the celebrities, while the miners got a sentence in the middle of the paper. The sagas of the celebrities were immensely comforting. They never seemed to suffer and seemed immune to the weeping plague that swept the globe. They remained pristine and endured only minor troubles and their lives seemed perfect.

The Hierarchy encouraged this focus on the famous. They were held up as exemplars of the myth of the garden. This was the myth of the great future that the people were working towards. The fact is no one ever saw the celebrities in the flesh. It never occurred to the populace, taken up with its own troubles, that the celebrities were not real.

28

One day, as Karnak was watching a flower-seller's shop, someone went past in a blur and said something which he heard only afterwards. When he spun round to see who it had been, he saw a man with a backpack striding away round the curve of the street.

'Shut up!' were the words he heard.

Karnak was puzzled by this because at the time he wasn't saying anything. He was just leaning silently against a lamp-post. He puzzled over it for an hour. Then he put it out of his mind, and went on watching the flower-seller's shop. Suddenly he felt different. He wasn't sure why. Then he realised that someone had put something in his hand. It was a single rose.

He was so shocked to see it that he dropped it as though it were burning. How had it got into his hand? He looked round and saw the slender back of a girl disappearing round the corner. He picked up the rose and ran after her. When he got to the corner he saw the girl vanish behind a building. But behind the building he saw her melt away into a field. In the field he saw her fade behind a tree. When he got to the tree he saw no one.

The roots of the tree were protruding from the ground. He sat down on the roots. He inhaled the fragrance of the rose as he sat. Soon he drifted into sleep.

29

Mirababa was led up the stone steps. Two of the old bards walked in front of him, and one behind. He climbed the steep steps and emerged onto the mountaintop. It was dawn. The sun had not yet risen but the air was diffused with a soft light. It was fresh and intoxicating and he breathed deeply.

With an overflowing heart, he gazed out onto the splendour of the world he saw from the mountaintop. The sea glittered far below. The green-brown edges of the islands shone in the faint light. The jagged shapes of the rock-faces emerged from the fading mist. He saw far into the distance. He saw the hills and the farmlands and the shimmering horizon.

He saw everything new minted, like a fresh new flower. He felt pure happiness with the clarity of a child. There was a new light in his head. A golden glow radiated from everything. He felt the limpid smile of the whole universe.

The sky was tender and blue. In the horizon he watched a roseate speck blossom out into the heavens. The three old bards silently watched the horizon with him, as if waiting for a sign. They watched in tranquil intensity. Mirababa was compelled to watch too. He didn't ask what he was watching for. He just watched. He watched with all his being.

As he watched the horizon, he watched himself. Something was rising in him. It was rising in its glory. The roseate hue filled the sky. The passion of the rose in the horizon became a kind of music in the sky. The bards watched with an unchanging intensity. Something magical, without a name, was rising in the boy. It brought a train of power. The rose in the horizon lost its shape. Then it spread and suffused the sky with beauty. Mirababa watched the blossoming red presence as it grew more concentrated. Then mysteriously, everywhere, something changed. The diffusion of the rose was complete.

Much time had passed as Mirababa and the old bards stood there on the mountainside, gazing at nothing on the horizon. Something unbearable, some intolerable paradox, something like pain that was also like bliss, something that was like death but was also like life, rose in Mirababa and overpowered him. He wanted to cry with holy joy. But suddenly, Mirababa beheld the magical disc of the sun, like a shy child peeking over a wall, revealing the tiniest bit of itself in the east.

At that exact moment the three bards burst into an incantation, and Mirababa, overwhelmed, dropped at their feet.

30

Among the forgotten myths of the world was one that told how all destinies are connected by an infinite web of light. The destiny of a stone on the side of a mountain is linked to the destiny of a woman in an office in the big city. A stream that meanders through a cold landscape of trees is connected to a bird soaring in the remote skies of the equator.

The myth tells of all things being born from one thing. In one variation, the thing is an egg. The egg split open and became night and day, heaven and earth, hard and soft, fire and water, earth and air. In another variation the thing was a seed in the great dark which opened out into universes. The seed was a seed of light and it fertilised the darkness with infinite forms. All the forms retained the light of the original seed.

In this myth if a person tugs at the thread of light of one thing all the other threads of light react and answer back. A sound was born in the silence and a thousand forms echoed. In the depths of the myth one of the seeds became an angel, and the angel became human.

But before being human man was a form of light in a circle of gold. Then one day this form of light conceived an unusual desire and fell from the circle of gold into a prison of flesh. But inside this prison of flesh was this form of light, this seed of the origin.

In another variation, man fell from the circle of dreams into the prison of history, from fable to fact.

In another variation the cosmic gourd was shattered and its fragments flew all over the universe, the mirror of the cosmos was broken and its fragments formed many worlds.

When you tug at one fragment of the original myth you pull all the others and there is a reaction in the universal linkage of things.

For centuries people destroyed fragments of the original mirror and pulverised fragments of the original gourd and nothing appeared to happen.

Then one day a rumbling is heard in the mountains and a quaking is felt underground, deep beneath our feet.

Then the infinite web of destinies begins to speak back.

31

When Mirababa awoke, the sun, a golden child, had risen. Dawn on the mountaintop was as beautiful as a dream. Clear were the lights of the sky, and pure was the lightness of its blue.

Without being told anything the boy knew that, as he beheld the world from the mountaintop, so must he behold his life and all life always.

He also knew that sometimes a perfect vision comes early. He sensed that he might never be on the mountaintop, or see this vision, or feel so happy and so pure again. He felt, paradoxically, that he was living the last day of his life.

The three bards with him had preserved a great silence, bearing themselves with dignity, strength, and lightness. They did not smile, yet were not grim. A benevolent gravity mantled everything they did. They were no longer staring at the eastern horizon.

One of them sat, looking down. The second stood, looking straight ahead. The third lay on the floor, gazing into the sky.

The boy understood that they were signs, a language. Their gestures were the high poems of the initiate.

Then the one who looked up rose and touched Mirababa on the shoulder, and began to descend the mountaintop. The one who looked straight ahead followed. The one who looked down brought up the rear.

After lingering a moment, gazing at the sea below, the birds wheeling above, and the rock-faces on the pyramidal mountain, Mirababa joined the three bards on their descent.

They began singing songs from the original myth as they went down from the mountaintop.

32

Karnak woke to find himself in a world he did not recognise. He was no longer sitting under a tree. He was in a dark place. It was very dark all around and for as far as he could see.

He sat up and felt what he was lying on. It felt square-shaped, it was of stone, and he surmised he had been sleeping on a cubic stone. He could see something of its whiteness in the dark.

He slid down from the stone and got to his feet. The earth felt solid enough, but in the dark he walked unsteadily, like a blind man without a stick. Where was he? He had no idea. In a warehouse? An underground crypt? A graveyard?

There were no stars above him, only darkness. After reaching for the darkness with outstretched hands, stumbling on the solid quality of the dark, he touched something substantial and reassuring. When he examined it with his hands he realised that he had merely found his way back to the stone.

As he touched its surface he came upon another familiar object. He could not see it but when he smelt it he realised it was the flower he had been holding before he fell asleep.

He climbed back onto the stone cube and lay down and tried to empty his mind of fear.

33

They were at the shrine. Mirababa was kneeling. The oldest of the bards held up an ancient sword, its haft the shape of a winged eagle. He saw along its blade inscriptions from the original myth. The bard held the sword above the boy's head.

Standing to the right of Mirababa was a bard in a white robe. He held up a heavy book resounding with incantations. The third bard stood to the left. He wore a crown of pentagrams.

The bard with the sword spoke:

'The time has come for you to leave. You have been raised to be a bard among us, but your destiny is not here. In accordance with the old man's wishes you will be allowed to read the book of the original myth. After you have read it you will leave our land and return only when you have fulfilled your destiny. None of us know what that destiny is. But come back only when it is done.'

The bard paused for a moment. There was a catch in his voice, as if he were concealing a strong emotion, but he mastered himself and continued:

'You will carry the book with you in your heart. The more of it you can remember on your first and only reading, the better it will be for you. Afterwards the book will be buried deep in the earth and not seen again for a thousand years.

Whatever you do we are with you. Carry the stone sarcophagus and the mountaintop always in your spirit.'

The bard slashed the air above Mirababa seven times. Then he tapped both shoulders with the flat of the blade. The bard with the book read solemnly from its pages. When he stopped reading the book went on incanting its lines.

Mirababa was led to the room of reflection. In the room there was a white table. On the white table there was a parchment manuscript. There was nothing else in the room except the fragrance of roses.

34

Many hours passed while Karnak lay on the cubic stone. Then gradually he became aware of presences in the darkness. He couldn't see anyone, but he could sense them. They were in a circle around him, watching him. He lay still and waited. He had no idea how long they had been there.

Then a voice said:

'What do you seek?'

Karnak sat up.

'I don't know.'

'Then why are you here?'

'I don't know.'

'How did you get here?'

'I don't know.'

There was a long silence. Then a woman's voice said:

'Do you know where you are?'

'No.'

A sterner voice said:

'You can't get here by accident. We are going to ask you the question one more time. What do you seek here?'

'I don't know where here is.'

'We can do nothing for you till you know what you are seeking here.'

'Where is here?'

'You must know.'

'How can I know?'
'That's your business. You must know, that's all.'

35

Mirababa became aware that the room was not what it seemed. There were no windows. There were no lamps, but there was light. He looked up at the ceiling. What he saw amazed him. He saw a heptagon within a heptagon. In it he saw the signs of the zodiac and the planets and the elements and the ancient letters of the alphabet which were tokens of magic and power, the letters with which the world was made.

In the centre of the heptagon was a rose. The magic letters formed the twenty-two petals of the rose. In the centre of the rose, a pure light, like the sun at dawn, streamed out. He didn't know how.

He looked at the floor and saw the same heptagon, with the signs of the planets, the zodiac, the elements, and the magic alphabet.

In a far corner of the room he noticed a strange door. It hadn't been there a moment ago.

In the centre of the room was a heptagonal altar. On each face was a golden plate with inscriptions from the original myth. Curious about the altar, Mirababa went towards it and touched it. To his surprise the altar moved sideways, revealing a white sarcophagus and upon it the miraculously preserved form of the great bard of the race. It was believed that he had written the original myth under divine inspiration.

The great father-bard lay there, preserved in a honey-coloured form, and he looked as if he were asleep. Long ago the father-bard had disappeared. No one knew where he had gone. Legend had it that he had not died, but had ascended into the skies in a white cloud.

Now here he lay, holding a book in one hand, and a sword in the other. There was a fresh rose on his heart.

Mirababa was astonished. When he entered the room it had been empty. He had no idea how the altar and the door and the father-bard came to be there. He felt the enchantment of the moment.

Then with reverence he recited from memory a few words from the original myth. As he recited the walls became seven and each wall was one of the seven colours.

He had discovered, without knowing it, the conjuring power of the word.

36

Karnak talked into the darkness. He spoke about the greatest loss of his life, how it had happened one day right before his eyes, and how he had been powerless to do anything, and how he despised himself for it. He poured out a lamentation, a rage against the times. He talked without end, in a circular purgatory, about the loss of the great love of his life. The darkness coagulated around him.

'I lost her when I was full of trust and innocence about the world,' he said. 'It is as if something in me died. I have not been able to think or feel or speak or even really exist because of all the confusion and the grief. I feel like I am dead. I feel like a shadow and I want more than anything else to be a living human being. I want to scream, but I don't know how. I know something is terribly wrong in the world, but I don't know what it is.'

His voice changed. He was not aware of what he was saying any more. The darkness he spoke into was very thick. He was no longer aware of himself. His voice rose in intensity, but not in volume. He spoke of blood on people's faces, blood in the streets, blood on the mouths of men and women, blood in the eyes of children. He spoke of lovers devouring one another when they kissed. He spoke of the horrors of daylight and the terrors of the night.

'I wander everywhere like a ghost,' he said. 'A ghost looking for its home.'

He looked around and still saw nothing. The darkness had become a thing, a wall. He felt it close to his face.

'I am lost and need help. I want to do something more than weep and wail at night. Something better than wandering about like a dead man in the day, knowing nothing, feeling nothing, sunk up to my neck in a nameless fear.'

He talked like this for a long time. The silence around him listened.

37

The seven colours pleased Mirababa. He sat down and with a clear mind began to read the manuscript the old man had left for him.

When he read he started to dissolve. The more he read the more he disappeared. When he was deep into the reading he was no longer there in the room. He was in another world. The words vanished from the page. Landscapes and people and stories took their place.

Phrases became icons in his mind. The words disappeared and became magic wands and changed the inner places in him. He glimpsed the obscure depths of the past. He peered into the murky mirror of beginnings. He saw how the prison came into being. He saw how each person became their own prison. He saw the long line of heroes, all of whom had tried to escape the prison, all of whom had perished in the attempt. Each one had left an immortal legacy, the tale of their attempt, the story of their incomplete discoveries. Each discovery had helped the next generation of heroes, each tale of a failed attempt had aided the next generation of brave ones.

He saw that the prison was built of the most indestructible material, that it was higher than the sky, deeper than the ocean, and wider than the whole world. He saw that the prison was the world and the world was the prison. He saw that an ageless Hierarchy ruled the world that was a prison. They had all the power. They seemed to know all that was going on everywhere. They were so powerful they were like gods. He saw that as nothing had any effect on the Hierarchy they were presumed indestructible. He saw that they were everywhere, in all lands, all villages. They were in the hills and the valleys and even in the depths of the sea.

He heard many things too. From the magic alphabets of which all things were made, great wisdom leapt out of the book and clung to his heart. He learnt of syllables that could alter reality. He learnt of incantations that could render things invisible. He saw the ten points through which the eternal power entered all things. He glimpsed an eternal inscription on an emerald tablet and understood in a flash its secret alchemical applications. He heard stories that regenerated the body and heart of man and woman. He heard the faintest whispers of the secret of eternal life.

Then, before he knew it, he was at the end of the book.

He felt as if he had lived innumerable lifetimes in vivid detail, as though he had been in epic battles, had several children and grandchildren, had crossed deserts, and had known poverty, great wealth, abominable fame, unbearable loneliness, ecstatic love, and abundant solidarity. He felt as if he had created an empire, squandered a fortune, loved uncountable women, suffered numberless heartbreaks, and watched many moons and magical dawns over mountains, cathedrals, rivers, peninsulas, and waterfalls. He felt as if he had been a whole race of people, lived out an entire people's history, and had been the living biography of legendary and unknown men and women. He felt as if he had died many times too, deaths as varied as each new day. He had died in a hospital ward, in his sleep, in a bath, by assassination, in the arms of loved ones, in rage, in joy. He felt also that he had been born many times too, and each birth was the same, coming again into the great prison of illusions.

All this he had experienced from reading the book. When he finished he felt that his mind was wiped clean. He felt empty and simple and light. He looked again at the manuscript.

It was only ten pages long.

38

Karnak finished talking. He could no longer separate himself from the darkness. While he was silent he felt he was the darkness. He listened to their listening. A long time passed during which he was no longer sure if there was anyone out there in the dark. Then he heard a voice say:

'You will be put through a series of tests. If you pass them we might let you take part in our great work. But we must warn you. Our work is not easy. You will have to be a hero every day. You will have to be creative in every way. You will have to think like a genius, live like a warrior, and be as loving as a saint.'

There was another long silence. The silence felt like a thing. It brushed up close to Karnak's face. It felt cold.

Then another voice spoke. A woman's voice.

'Never will it be revealed to you who we are or how our order works. Our work is too great for any one person to know anything but a small part of it. Who we are is unimportant. We will reach you through dreams and in unusual ways.'

Her voice died away gently. In the silence that followed he heard water running faintly in the distance. He couldn't be sure if he was imagining it. Soon the sound faded. He strained, but heard nothing. The nothing felt like a thing. It brushed up close against the skin on the back of his neck. It felt like the caress of gentle breathing.

Then another voice broke in on him, the voice of a man. He seemed to be speaking from a height.

'You will recognise us by many signs. It might be a rose, or a fable, or a book. It could also be a song, a fragrance, or a smile.'

He paused. When he spoke again his voice seemed to come from somewhere else, neither high nor low.

'Remember there are many false flowers, false books, false smiles. If you are deceived, that's your business. If you are caught, you know what awaits you, a darkness worse than death, a hell in prison.'

The voice dropped away and another voice took over. It was the strong voice of a woman and she spoke fast as if she wanted to raise his heartbeat to the level of mild panic.

'You will be returned to your life. Nothing will have changed, but everything has changed for you. Pay attention to everything. Your initiation will be concealed in seemingly ordinary things. If you sustain your course, if you keep your faith, then you might find, in one way or another, that which you have lost. But first we must destroy the existing order of the world. Till then you must live and behave as normal. You must be normal.'

Then with a slight rustle, as of silk, and a gentle movement in the dark, like a breeze from an open door, they were gone.

He lay there in the dark, on the cubic stone, trying not to think. Then he picked up the flower again, and inhaled its mysterious fragrance of the east.

39

You are born into prison. You spend your whole life there. It is hard work. There is no relief. You earn your living. You live. Maybe you raise a family. Every day you work. Living is work. Your holidays are in prison.

Sometimes you look at the sky and dream of freedom. But what does freedom mean when your whole life is a prison? You dream of escape, but to escape is to escape into prison. Everything you learn is in prison and is about prison. The bars are invisible. They are made of your flesh. You have been here so long that you think prison is everything. You think that prison is all there is.

But every now and again a rumour comes to you. The rumour says that there is a life beyond prison, that prison is not all there is. The rumour says that there is something beyond. There is no proof of this.

There have been legends through the ages of people who found something beyond. The legends speak of a garden and mountains and seas and emerald stones. The legends speak of happiness and love and freedom. No one has any proof of these things. There are no pictures. There are no images. No one has gone and come back with proof of what lies beyond.

For you prison is all there is because it is all you know. Prison is all anyone knows or has ever known. For many it is the only truth they will deal with. The rest is wishful thinking and legends.

You live your life in prison and when you die you come back to prison and begin your sentence all over again. You do this without hope, without dreams of freedom. You do this in the prison in which all you see is all there is.

40

Mirababa was led to the edge of things by the three bards. With nothing but fragments of the original myth in his mind, he left the realm he had known.

Then he set off into the labyrinth of the world.

41

Karnak woke to find himself under the tree. He had the strange feeling that he had spent his life wandering about in a cursed world. The tree under which he sat was in blossom. He stared at the canopy of whiteness above him.

His head felt clearer than it had done all his life. A heaviness had left his heart. The flower was still in his hand. Looking at it gave him the absurd hope that one way or another he would be reunited with his lover.

For the first time since that fatal morning, he felt the full force of his grief. It was as though he had woken from a spell. He began crying but at the same time he was smiling.

Sometimes she would sit in his room and would be still, lost in meditation. She would be like that for a long time. After a while a faint light shone around her. It shook him a little.

'What are you thinking about when you're gone like that?' he asked once.

'About all that is possible,' she replied, and was silent again.

BOOK THREE

1

Ruslana had watched him from the darkness. She noticed that he no longer sought the fields at night. She had watched him at his window. He was always looking out, as if waiting for someone. She watched him as he walked down the streets in the day. She watched him as he suddenly burst into tears while walking. He would weep in the street, overcome by an unknown grief. All this moved Ruslana deeply, but she made no attempt to contact him.

She had found her way to the underground movement. She had been part of the signs that appeared in the ordinary world. For a long time now she had rejected the world of wailing, of the Hierarchy. She had rejected the world in which it was better to be dead than alive.

For Ruslana there was only one goal in life. There was only one great goal worth living for, to overthrow the Hierarchy, destroying that tyranny. She wanted more than anything to rid the world of their omnipotent control.

It was an impossible goal and she knew it. But there was nothing else worth doing. To overthrow the Hierarchy was almost as impossible as escaping from the prison of the world. But escaping from the prison of the world was not her dream. Overthrowing the powers that tyrannise the lives of all people, this was her dream.

She did not even dream of love. For the oppression of life,

the universal wailing, the great unknown misery of living, these made love impossible. How can one love in an air so poisoned? How can one love in a world without hope? These were questions she asked herself.

The old myths taught to her in childhood by her father still resonated in Ruslana. She believed that the Hierarchy could be overthrown not with violence, but with the co-ordinated power of the underground, the force of mysteries.

2

She would sometimes steal into the world and listen to the songs in the madhouses. There was no sweeter singing in the churches, the opera houses, or the concert halls than the voices that sang at night in the madhouses.

They were not called madhouses. They were called Regeneration Centres.

There were now more madhouses than cinemas or schools. They increased in number every day. Within their walls could be heard stories told in hushed voices. Strange philosophies were whispered there under the trees. Ruslana would go under the shadow of the walls and listen to the mad reciting banished words from the old myths. It seemed to her that the last wisdom left in the world was in the madhouses.

She watched each day as white vans brought new people. One evening she listened at the wall as a woman recounted how she had been unable to sleep and had found herself wailing at dawn and had gone to see her psychiatrist.

'I confessed to dreams in which I was burning down the world. When the session was over the door opened and a uniformed man led me out of the building and into the van. I did not complain. I think I deserve to be here. It is better here than out there, don't you think?'

'That's why I am here,' someone else said.

'We can read books here and they'll only think we're mad.'

'Every night I dreamt of escape and I never knew where to escape to, till I came here.'

Then they began singing.

She liked to linger outside the walls and listen to the singing and the stories of the mad. There was a cherry tree near the wall. Ruslana would sit under the tree sometimes and wait. The wind brought songs and she noted down the words. She paid attention when she heard people exchanging dreams they'd had. She noted down the dreams too.

The inmates seemed to like coming to the walls just as much as she did, even though they were inside. Maybe the reason they liked coming to the walls was that after she had listened to their songs and their dreams she would hurl a cluster of flowers over the wall. Then she would steal away.

3

The songs and dreams she had noted down were taken to the underworld. Distilled from them, over time, were the images and words which appeared mysteriously in the world.

She knew there were many like her noting down the dreams and songs of the mad, the lamentations and the wailings of the oppressed. She didn't know who they were. No one knew who the others were. But she recognised them in the fleeting smiles she encountered in the world.

4

She often went to the farms and listened to the despondent songs of the women hoeing and carrying, the men digging and planting. She listened to the dreams of workers and peasants and noted them down. The songs were always sad.

In the villages and in the countryside they wailed at night as much as they did in the city. In remote hamlets and in villages on the mountaintops those who did not wail at night, who slept peacefully, were visited by the authorities and taken away to the dark place that no one knows.

Those left behind, who wailed in their sleep, dreamt of farmlands where human bodies were planted. Corpses grew from the earth like grotesque vegetation.

5

Ruslana watched the women of the world grow weirder. They grew pale, their faces harder and their eyes colder. Their voices became scratchy and taut. They sought love everywhere with blazing eyes and were suspicious of love with their frightened hearts. She saw women filled with worries, filled with fear. Those that were rich had more leisure to be neurotic. Those that were poor were neurotic because they were poor. Those who were happy were happy briefly before returning to their abundant worries. Pleasures among them were brief and intense; repentance long and agonised.

She saw how the women distrusted men. They saw men as barbarians. They hated and feared and resented them. They were baffled by men, provoked by them, and fascinated by this parallel species that shared their world of worries and wailing.

She saw how people in crowds were locked in their heads, locked in the prisons they carried about with them.

6

Every now and then there appeared someone who was a little unusual. Such a person might stop one day in the middle of the street and wonder what had stopped them. They might realise that they had been stopped by a question.

Every now and then a man or woman would ask themselves that question; and from that moment on they would be different. It would be as if they had eaten of the tree of knowledge. A profound unease would creep into them. Being awake would be one long silent question. They would begin to look at everything with altered eyes. A haunted expression would appear on their faces. They would suddenly wake in the depths of the night and hear an inexplicable cry. They would begin to wonder if the world had changed overnight and become tinged with a nightmarish quality or whether it was they who had changed.

They might see strange patches on the faces of their colleagues. They might notice how people bled when they kissed and notice that children had distorted eyes. They might notice blood leaking out of the food they ate, from the apples and the oranges, from the carrots and the rice. They might notice the multiplication of flower shops and notice that no one ever bought flowers there. They might catch glimpses of figures in the dark as they disappeared and they would afterwards find stencilled on the streets, painted on walls, or branded on billboards the words:

UPWAKE! or UPRISE! or UPSIDEDOWN!

They would notice gaps in the world and then see the gaps filled up with madhouses, hospitals, cemeteries. They would wander away from people. They would be more alone, would talk to imaginary children, and sit at the foot of trees. They would find themselves weeping without cause. Then they would notice the fleeting figures more often. They would be obsessed with the signs and words. And then one day a loved one that they had not paid proper attention to, because of all the pressures of life, would suddenly disappear, or be taken away, or would begin raving wildly at dawn and couldn't be stopped.

They would begin to seek. They would go from place to place seeking some mysterious balm or elixir hidden in the darkening world. Then just when they thought it all too much, could bear it no longer, and were about to give up forever, lying at the root of a tree, they might find in their hand a flower. Ruslana might have given it to them. They might smell the flower and find themselves lying in the darkness, on a cubic stone.

But it happened very rarely.

7

Karnak felt that something in him had changed. He didn't notice it at first and didn't know what it was.

He began to pay attention to small things. Where previously he had noticed the expression on people's faces, now he noticed their eyes, or their shadow, or the darkness that surrounded them.

Then he was surprised to see people he knew walking down the road, asleep. He had never noticed this phenomenom before. Now he saw it at the markets, the banks, in crowds, or when people were crossing busy roads. He was shocked to see that though their eyes were wide open, though they talked, looked at their watches, hailed a cab, engaged in arguments, they were in fact fast asleep.

For a while he was not sure if he was imagining it. He wondered how he could put it to the test. There was a shop near him where he often went for his provisions. The shop was run by a gentleman and his two daughters. Every time he went in the bell jingled and a head would appear above the counter. He wondered what they did below it.

Then one day he went to the shop and, as silently as he could, he opened the door and went in and peeked behind the counter. The man was reading a newspaper with his eyes wide open but he was fast asleep.

Karnak went back out. He opened the door and the bell jingled and the man's head popped up.

'Ah, it's you,' he said. 'I was just dreaming about you.'

'Really?' Karnak said. 'What was the dream about?'

'Nothing really.'

'Please, tell me.'

'I dreamt that you were in the newspaper I was reading.'

'What was I doing?'

'You were trying to get me to wake up. You were talking to me inside the newspaper.'

'You mean like a speaking newspaper?'

'Yes, something like that.'

'That's an invention for the future.'

'But I dreamt it now, just before you came in.'

'But were you asleep?'

'No. I was just reading the newspaper.'

'But you said…'

'Never mind. Everything's a bit confusing, even to me. What can I do for you?'

The young lover decided not to press it. He bought a bar of soap and went home.

Ever since then he noticed bank tellers asleep while counting money, doctors asleep while conducting intricate operations, judges asleep in court during significant murder trials, drivers asleep at the wheels of their cars, and workers asleep drilling the roads.

Karnak grew disturbed. Had they been asleep all this time, all his life, or was it a recent thing? How could he be sure they were asleep? And if they were asleep and made the world function, made civilisation run on its wheels, then is it not possible that being asleep is the right and natural condition of the world? Would that not mean that not being asleep was unnatural and therefore counter to the smooth running of the world? What was more alarming to him was this question: was he asleep or not?

8

When did he first become aware that the world was run by people who were asleep? If Karnak were to trace the first moment of this awareness, he would say it was the day he woke up under the tree, with the rose in his hand. That day he had begun weeping for his lost lover. He had wept for seven days without cease.

It got so bad that he found the weeping was taking possession of him. His normal moments were when he wept. Abnormality was when he wasn't weeping. Then after seven days his weeping ceased. On the seventh day he wept but no tears poured down his face. His tear ducts were exhausted.

After the weeping a strange calm came over him. Gradually he became aware that thoughts were deserting his mind. Vast spaces opened in him. He would often fall asleep and find himself wandering in a great empty expanse. He would wander for days and encounter no one and nothing. The nothingness horrified him. He couldn't get away from it. He couldn't escape it. Then the nothingness, like an erasing wind, entered into him. He began screaming and couldn't stop.

When he woke up he felt his interior world had expanded and in that expansion there was nothing. He had no sense of who he was and yet he felt he was everyone. He was everybody. This alarmed him.

All this time he stayed at home. He stayed at the window

and looked out. He looked out vacantly. He felt as vast and as empty as the sky. He lost his desire to wander, to search for those who could give him answers. He sat at a table, before the window, and simply stared.

One morning when he woke himself with screaming he decided a walk might help. He hadn't been outdoors for weeks.

He got dressed, went out, and sought the rich variety of humanity. He sought crowds. As he plunged into the gatherings in the parks and wandered through the markets his mind began to stir. He walked gingerly. He felt like someone from another planet, or a new-born baby staggering about in an adult body.

In the park, in a crowd, he caught a glimpse of a girl's exquisite face. She had a rose in her hair. She was holding a placard in her hands which read:

'The people who run this world are all ASLEEP.'

He read the placard in a flash and then it was obscured by the crowd. In that flash he saw the girl's smile. It was like a tender electric shock, and it startled him.

But before he could recover and seek her out Karnak was engulfed in the crowd. When he fought his way out, the girl and the placard were gone. He asked people around him if they'd seen the girl or the placard. No one had seen her. No one had noticed such a thing as a placard.

9

That was the beginning of Karnak's uncertainty about the world. There were times when he would stare out of the window and not be sure he wasn't staring out of a dream. Sometimes wandering the streets he was struck with the sense that nothing around him was real.

This feeling was so strong that on some evenings he would stand in the middle of a park and gaze at the trees and the grass and the sky and the distant buildings and the swings and the towers of the city and have a notion that it was all a gigantic stage set.

He felt the houses and the streets and the vehicles and the trees and the cranes in the city were all unstable. He felt the instability of it all.

He felt that the people he passed in the streets were figures in a dream.

Then it occurred to him faintly that he too was asleep and that his whole life and every waking and sleeping hour of it was all a dream.

10

This sense of being asleep while being awake so bothered him that he didn't let himself think about it. His vacancy remained. It may have been because of his vacancy that he experienced everything as being unreal.

There wasn't much he could do about his vacancy. He woke into it and got up and lived his day in vacancy. He stared without registering, listened without thinking, and yet he was not porous to life.

Something in his mind had changed. It had expanded to include an empty dark space in which nothing dwelt except an endless wind.

But there were moments when it seemed he glimpsed something real. These moments were so fleeting as to be almost not registered. Walking in the street, crossing a road, gazing at the skyscrapers and the high-rise buildings, he would catch a glimpse of a strangely beautiful and familiar face, a smiling face. Before he knew it, the face would be gone.

Where had he seen that face before? His memory yielded nothing. He would stop walking and he would look round. He would hurry in the direction of the face and not find it. Then he would lean against a lamp-post and weep.

Much later, at home, while contemplating a crescent moon from his window, the face would come back to him. Then he remembered it was the face of Amalantis.

11

Ruslana always knew that the world was run by people who are asleep. Her father had shown her this secret when she was a child. It was as astonishing as the discovery of colours on the wings of a butterfly.

Her father had told her to shut her eyes and had taken her to a distant realm. When she opened her eyes in that realm she found herself in a familiar world.

'Look at the people,' her father had said.

She looked and saw people that she knew. People in the streets, people at work, men directing traffic, women drilling at the sides of roads, the newspaper vendors, and the market traders. They were all asleep. They slept while doing their jobs. They worked efficiently. Everywhere this was true.

When her father brought her back to this world, she was overcome with curiosity. She went about with her father and she looked at people. She looked at everything. She noticed, for the first time, that everything was the opposite of what she had been taught, the opposite of what she had seen before.

She wanted to tell her father that she had seen people who were asleep in their beds but who were wandering about. She had seen people who were wandering about but who were asleep. She wanted to say that she thought that walls and trees and houses and the earth and cars were all solid. But they were all shadows and they were all made of millions of little dots. The air which she thought was empty was full of a kind of universal liquid which flowed everywhere and which glowed with light. She told her father these things. He smiled at her. She said:

'How can they be asleep and awake at the same time?'

'They're awake because they have life and consciousness. They're asleep because they don't know who they are.'

'How can they be both?'

'Because they are.'

'Are they asleep or awake?'

'They're asleep.'

'But they walk about. They do things, they talk, they cry, they get married, don't they?'

'Yes, they do all that, but asleep.'

'I don't understand.'

'Yes, you do.'

'Then I don't understand my understanding.'

'You don't need to. Just remember what you saw.'

Through all the changes of the years, through the horrors, the wailings, the deaths, she never did forget what she saw. But what she saw grew in significance within her with the passing years.

12

I t was her father who started Ruslana on the path that led underground. Her father had remained something of a mystery to her. All she knew about him was that he kept alive in secret one strand of the ancient myths. He was a protector of the word.

He lived a shadowy life. He read books. He read to her as a child from books which, with the new dispensation, had disappeared from the world. The books he read from were very peculiar. They were books that could change. They changed whatever they encountered.

One of her father's books was at the same time a kingdom, a universe, a tablet, a room, a street, a pair of spectacles, a computer, a dream, a rope, a history, and a river.

Once her father took her swimming in the river of the book. It was a luminous river, its banks undulating. They went sailing in a boat with a red sail. He read to her lines from the river, lines that became flowers on the shore, lines that became fishes. They swam in the river that day and her father took her down to the bottom of the river, to a coral reef, and to a cave. In the cave she had a vision. Dripping with lustrous water, they stepped out of the river that was a book and dried themselves and then she found herself listening to a magic tale, read to her in the evening by her father.

Another of her father's books was at the same time an

oracle, the memory of a race, an obstacle course, a forest, a mirror, a television, a prophecy, a pyramid, and a village.

Another of his books was at the same time a temple, a mountain, the planet Sirius, a hall of records, the bright city of Aketaten, and a sacred province in Atlantis.

Her father's books were not read in a normal way. Some of them were read with the hands. Some were read by placing them at the centre of the forehead. One of the books could only be read with eyes closed. Another one could only be read in dreams, while the reader was asleep, with the book under the pillow.

There was a very special book of her father's which could only be read by the dead. It was placed in their coffins, over the heart.

There was one book that was only read by drinking. Water was poured on its waterproof pages and the water was drunk. The words filled out in the blood and heart and brains, till the reader became the words.

There was another special book that was read in the wind. The book was left dangling, the wind blew its pages, and the reader, with the light on their face, read the words which the wind dispersed.

One of her father's favourite books was the one that was read only by writing it. But this book was such a great mystery that only initiates were allowed, by participation, to penetrate its pages.

13

Ruslana's path to the underworld began with a word.

She sat one day at a window, learning to read from the magic pages of the book which the wind scattered. After months of no success she saw a vision of gold speeding towards her from the sun. She shut her eyes, but saw the vision more brightly. As it came close to her the vision changed into a face. She opened her eyes to see it better and a burst of music swelled in her heart at the glimpse of a face that changed into a single word which she did not understand.

She took the word to her father in his library. It must have been the mood of the library which did it, but as she entered with the word in her hand, the word changed back into light.

Her father looked up and said:

'I see you've found a word.'

'What does it mean?'

'Its meaning changes. It's your word now. It'll change and reveal things to you when needed.'

'But how can I understand it?'

'Don't try. The word will be your guide and friend. It'll do the work. All you have to do is listen.'

'It seems so precious. Where should I keep it?'

'Keep it where you like. You can wear it round your neck, like a pendant. You can swallow it. You can keep it in your heart, or you can nestle it in the middle of your forehead. Use your imagination.'

'Okay, I'll do that.'

'What?'

'You'll see.'

With an air of mystery, she left her father's library. She went to her room and took down the book which the wind reads. She held the word which the sun had given her and placed it right in the middle of her forehead. When she looked in the mirror the bright word had gone.

That night when she slept she was sure that she had three eyes. With the third eye in the middle of her forehead she saw that the people who run the world are all asleep. She also saw again the face she had seen before the face became the word. It was a face she would never forget. It was a face which later she would seek in secret throughout the world.

14

Ruslana grew to understand with the passing of the years that the word she had put into her forehead was not a word in the normal sense. It was more than a word. It was a light and a darkness. It was a hunger and the satisfaction of that hunger. It was a quest, a wound, a cure, a love story, a longing, a fragment of eternity. It was an abyss, a splinter, a gentle madness, a wildness, a wailing, a profound peace, a great unrest. It was not a word but a destabilisation, a harmony, a death, a birth, a constellation, a burning star. The word expanded in her brain and possessed her heart.

One day the word sprouted in her heart and she gave a great cry and rushed to her father in his library. She was shocked to find him hovering in the air, with nothing holding him up. He came down gently to the ground but the sight of it paralysed her voice.

For seven days she was unable to utter a word. Then her father gave her water poured over the pages of the mysterious water-book. As soon as she drank her tongue uncleaved itself from her palate and she forgot what she was going to say. By then she had also forgotten what she had seen.

'What did you want to tell me, Ruslana?' her father asked.

'I've forgotten.'

'No, you haven't. It has to do with your heart.'

'I think the word has gone to my heart,' she said, with tears in her eyes.

'Good,' her father said. 'Good.'

With that he turned his attention to a piece of music which began playing from a book which he opened. The music soothed her heart and the pain vanished with its soaring cadences.

15

The word grew in her till she found herself understanding things that she had not learnt. She found herself understanding books that had before seemed too difficult for her. She understood philosophical concepts which had puzzled her, like the infinity continuum. She understood expressions on people's faces, understood their moods, and even understood what they were trying to say, or what they thought, whether they had expressed it or not.

She understood that the world was not what it seemed. She understood that reversal was the way. She understood that the truth of things was upside down. She grasped that those who thought they knew were ignorant, that those who thought they had power were powerless, and that those who thought they knew themselves were in great darkness.

She was surprised at the understanding that grew in her. Without knowing how, she learnt that all the stories she had been told concealed secret stories. She understood that the new myths concealed the old. She realised that to read the truth in the world required a bending of the mind, even the silencing of thought.

She found that she could look at symbols and they would speak to her. They would teach her things. A triangle taught her how to paint. A square taught her how to defend herself. A pentagram taught her how to find the essence of things.

A circle taught her that she was part of all aspects of the universe.

Colours taught her things as if speaking with an audible voice. She found in red a portal to vitality, in blue a portal to tranquillity, in green a portal to all nature.

The word grew in her till it became her own inner academy, filling her with intuitions, with knowledge, and with an essential grasp of obscure and arcane wisdom.

16

Then one day her father did something so shocking that she was ill for days afterwards. She had been staring for a long time at a butterfly and it gave her such odd notions that she had gone to her father's library. Before she could begin to say what was on her mind her father spoke.

What he said changed her life the moment he said it; and propelled her, in due course, to the underground.

'This world,' he said, 'is a prison. My dear Ruslana, it is a prison that you must transcend.'

'A prison?'

'Yes.'

'How?'

'How what?'

'How is it a prison?'

'Can you escape your body?'

'No.'

'Can you escape death?'

'No.'

'Can you escape suffering?'

'No.'

'Are you only your body?'

'I don't know.'

'Do you feel something in you that is not just your body?'

'Yes.'

'What?'

'My emotions.'

'What else?'

'My dreams.'

'What else?'

'My thoughts.'

'What else?'

'I don't know. Something in me that is aware, that watches, that listens. Something deep and still and nameless. And when I am happy it seems to be very great.'

'So you are not just your body?'

'No.'

Her father was silent.

'But you said this world is a prison.'

'Which you must transcend.'

'The world or my body?'

'You experience the world in your body. You suffer and enjoy the world in your body. You can't escape the world and you can't escape your body. If you could it wouldn't be a prison.'

'How can I transcend it then?'

'You must find a way.'

'Why?'

'Because you will experience the same things over and over again.'

'Can I escape through death?'

'No. Death is another part of the prison.'

'Can I escape through drugs?'

'Drugs only make you more imprisoned.'

'How can I escape then?'

'Not escape. Transcend.'

'How can I transcend?'

'In life.'

'In life?'

'It can only be done in life. Here, now, in your consciousness, while you are alive.'

'How?'

'Find a way.'

'Have you found a way?'

'We're not talking about me.'

'Why not?'

'Because sooner than you think I won't be here any more. I want you to listen, to pay attention.'

She was quiet. She became still.

'The world is full of signs,' he said. 'Some of the signs are sent to help you find your way. Most people pay no attention to the signs because they have not been taught to see them. They are taught that there is nothing to see. They are kept blind. But pay attention.'

He paused.

'Listen with your heart and your wisdom. The world is a prison which you must transcend. Then you will know true freedom and you will find that it is very different to what anyone has ever said.'

17

Ruslana was ill after that for seven days. It began simply enough. Her father had finished speaking. A long silence had followed. Then she remembered the butterfly she had been staring at and it occurred to her that there was a relationship between notions she got from the butterfly and her father's remarks. She went back to the window where she had been following the butterfly with her eyes, but found that it was dead. It had died on the windowsill.

Later that day she buried it and thought nothing of it. That night she dreamt she was trapped in a butterfly's body. She didn't know how she got there. She flew everywhere, with all her strength, seeking someone who could free her from the butterfly's body. She flew across the ocean and came to the house of a magician. He sat on a golden carpet. He had a long moustache and fierce eyes. He said:

'I can free you from the butterfly on one condition.'

'What is that?'

'That you give me the word that you have in the middle of your forehead.'

'I can't give you that.'

'Then I can't free you from the butterfly.'

'I will give you anything else.'

'I don't want anything else. I only want the word.'

'Why do you want it?'

'Because I have everything I need to attain immortal life except that word.'

'But it's my word.'

'I've been looking for my word all my life and never found it. I've never found anyone else who has found their word either. You are the only one. If you give it to me I will free you from the butterfly's body.'

'I can't do that.'

'Then you must remain a butterfly, till someone kills you.'

'Who?'

'Me, for example.'

With that remark, the magician caught the butterfly and shut it away in a cup, and shut the cup away in a dark cave. At this point she woke up shivering.

The next day she fell ill. She had several dreams. In some she was trying to escape from a narrow prison of rock. In another she was in a narrow corridor. Then in a nut-shell. And then she was in a room made of lead with no doors or windows. It was the room of sorrow.

On the seventh day she dreamt of a butterfly soaring into the sun. She awoke hungry and weak. The house was empty. She went to her father's library and found that all his books were gone.

18

Change came swiftly into Ruslana's life. One day she was a girl with bad dreams and the next she was a girl whose father was a fugitive. He had become a wanted man. In secret, they fled the house of her childhood.

They moved houses several times. They slept in fields, by the wayside, or in hay lofts. They lived in the countryside, in abandoned farms. She remembered times when, under nocturnal rain, they slept on a hillside.

Then they changed their identities and returned to the great city. Incognito, in hiding, her father set up an invisible bookshop and lived in silence. The books were invisible. He began his research into lost masterpieces. His clientele was discreet. Then he set up a secret publishing house that disseminated books stealthily, against the laws of the land. Many of the books were meant to be destroyed after being read. Anyone found with a book tended to disappear.

Soon writers appeared in the house. They wanted to write, but there was nowhere to do it, so her father gave them shelter. He fed, clothed, and looked after them. He arranged constantly changing accommodations for them. In verse, in dramas, in novels, and short stories, they wrote the history of the times. They were the last writers left in the world, the last dreamers.

They wrote with the consciousness of the death of a great

tradition. When they woke up in the morning they began writing and they wrote all through the day. They took no breaks. They wrote in a magic language. The original common language they wrote with when they first arrived became transformed in their contact with her father's invisible and magical books.

Each writer found a few syllables, fragments of a word from the book which the wind dispersed. Each writer was changed by time spent in the new underground library which her father had reconstructed. In that shady, dark and unprepossessing house the lost traditions, the forgotten stories, and the fading legends were reconstituted and redreamt by the last of the earth's writers. They rewrote while keeping exactly the same *The Odyssey, One Thousand and One Nights*, the *Epic of Gilgamesh*, the *Bhagavad Gita*, the *Tao Te Ching*, and hundreds of novels, poems, plays, fables, philosophies and imaginings, lost to the human race.

They redreamt them anew, in a magic language that expressed in one word what the old language expressed in a thousand. Tirelessly they recreated the lost library of the human race. Then they began the narrative of the times. They wrote stories both public and private, the intimate tales of hidden sufferings and triumphs, the narratives of disappearance, the poetic transcriptions of the world-wide wailing.

Ruslana not only witnessed all these changes in her life, she grew with them.

19

The word Ruslana had put into her forehead grew with her. She would often hear a whisper in her head. She would listen and then it would be gone. Sometimes when she slept she caught a glimpse of that face which had accompanied the arrival of the word.

She was manning the shop one day, alone, when someone came in like the wind and left a flower on the table in front of her and then vanished. This was so strange she told her father about it.

'Let me see the flower,' he said.

She showed him the rose, and he smiled.

'You have been contacted by the underground. From now on be alert and be prepared for anything.'

'Like what?'

'Anything.'

'Are we going to move again?'

'I don't know.'

'What is the underground?'

'They'll tell you in good time.'

'How do you know about this?'

'I know all kinds of things.'

'Like what?'

'Mysteries.'

'When will they contact me?'

'When they're ready.'

'What are the mysteries?'

'They'll find you when you're ready.'

'When will I be ready?'

'No one knows.'

She waited and time passed and nothing happened. There were no further developments for a long time. This silence intrigued her. She began to research the underground. She learnt that it had nothing to do with trains, the Greek under-world, or the Egyptian underworld, or the land of the dead. She learnt that it could also be called the underground or the underworld. It had nothing to do with crime syndicates, spirits, or political resistance. It had nothing to do with witch-craft or anything of darkness. She found out what it wasn't, but she didn't find out what it was.

Her father, taken up with the mysteries, did not enlighten her. He was busier than ever with his secret occupations, with the magic books, the word, various procedures of enchant-ment, and bringing together fragments of the original myth.

But his hints and unfinished sentences only made her more fascinated with the underground. Her fascination got her nowhere. There was no information to be found anywhere about the nature of the underground.

It became clear to her after some time that all she could do was wait.

20

One of her father's pet projects was a holographic exhibition of the world's lost masterpieces. His dream was to assemble the lost great dreams, the great novels and poems and essays and myths and plays and stories. He wanted to recreate, in a magic space, the lost library of the human race. He wanted it to be an exhibition of lost notions, lost ideas, lost concepts.

Since the destruction of books and the banishing of libraries the memories of people had become short. No one remembered that there were once people who dreamt and embarked on fabulous adventures, people of bold imaginations and daring hearts. Then after a generation no one knew what had been done or dreamt before. Very few knew that they were heirs to conceptions of genius. They saw their highest achievements in the day's newspapers, in the latest popular songs and the latest fashions.

Books were no longer a memory. They were not even a rumour. The new myths, circulated in the air, through electronic dreams, made the world seem recent.

Her father wanted to raise the sunken Atlantis of books. But as books were forbidden the only thing he could do was show the dream of books. Painstakingly, amidst his numerous other undertakings, he created a veritable universe of lost masterworks. Each page shimmered in its holographic brilliance.

At a touch the world of the artist came to life. At another touch the words sang into the air, resuscitated by ancient voices. Original parchment, forgotten alphabets, old papyri, vellum texts with ancient calligraphy magically appeared in the air before the viewer. Sometimes, quivering in space, was the artist himself, the artist herself, wistful and vaporous, like a ghost summoned from a long Elysian rest.

'Why are you doing this?' Ruslana would ask.

'In these times, all we can do is be a sign,' her father replied.

'But won't it get you into trouble?'

'We're in trouble anyway. No one can live in peace in times like this. We have to help to bring about the end of the world.'

'The end?'

'Yes, the end.'

'Why?'

'So that a new beginning can begin. But first there must be an end.'

'How?'

'How what?'

'How do we bring about the end?'

Her father laughed. It was a rare laughter.

'All these things you will know for yourself. Sooner than you think, I will no longer be here. You must learn to rely on yourself, to trust the guidance of your light. You must be a sign.'

'A sign of what?'

'The end. The beginning.' He looked at her. 'A sign for the world to wake up and arise. A sign of magical revolution, the revolution of the spirit.'

'How can I be a sign of so much?'

'With simplicity.'

'I wish I knew how.'

'You will find a way. I have complete faith in your light.'

'I wish I did,' the girl said, with a touch of sadness.

21

Sometimes at night Ruslana had intimations of the horrors to come. In her sleep, she would be taken to places where those who disappeared wandered in a bleak and interminable landscape. They wandered through thirst and infernal hunger till there was nothing left in them, till the flesh fell off them. They crawled even as they became a bundle of bones. Afterwards their skeletons went on wandering in the endless plains of sorrow.

She had no idea who they were. Each one wandered alone. Vast and bleak as the place was, they never came across one another. It was a place without memory, without sound, without water. Hundreds of thousands wandered in those bleak plains and perished without anyone knowing. She heard only the faint wailing in the wind after their skeletons had crumbled to dust.

Sometimes in the night she saw the bodies of the disappeared bundled into giant furnaces. She saw people shot in empty alleys. She saw a great darkness, like the forms of the dead, steal into houses and drag out sleeping inhabitants. She told her father what she saw.

'As I feared,' he said. 'You can protect a child from evil, but not from the truth.'

It was only later Ruslana understood what he meant. Only later, when she had to face the furnace of reality, did she realise she had been protected in the Aladdin's Cave of her father's powers.

Though the house was poor and run-down, the outside world never intruded on them. The evils of the world went past their home without imprinting themselves on her waking mind. But sometimes at night she knew that her time in the garden of her father's love was going to end.

Once when she was asleep she saw her father walking backwards into a mirror. The next morning he took her down to the basement and opened a book as large as the wall. Then holding her hand, he stepped with her into the spaces between the lines of the giant book. With a gasp she saw the shimmering river and knew it to be the oldest river in the universe. Everything was touched with a beautiful light. The trees, the flowers, the grass lay in this silky light of the beginning of time. In the air, near her face, was the dead butterfly. It was alive and bright with the fresh colours of its first arrival.

'What world is this?' she cried in exultation.

'This is the real world.'

'What world are we living in?'

'That is the world of those who are asleep.'

'So this is the real world?'

'Yes, the world after the end.'

In the distance Ruslana saw a temple on a hill. It made a harmonious shape. She looked at the undulating landscape. Far below there were the steeples, the rooftops, the obelisks, the beautiful structures of the city. She half-expected to see a unicorn.

'Unicorns don't belong here,' her father said, reading her thought. 'They belong to another world.'

She heard music from across the river. A boat drifted past. Two lovers lay on its deck, reading to each other in sweet voices. A dog barked behind a tree. Round the knoll, on the grass, young musicians were practising a concerto one of them had written. In the sky a giant balloon sailed past. In the huge basket which the balloon bore, a group of friends were laughing and waving at something. On the balloon was the legend: 'I LOVE.' In a grove of trees children were playing and laughing. Their voices sounded from the leaves.

'It's time to go back,' her father said.

'Why?'

'I wanted you to see that a beginning is possible,' he said, not answering her question. 'I want you to remember this when the times become unbearable, when it seems as though it would be better to be dead, and when you have no one to comfort you, except my voice in your head.'

With that they stepped back into their house, and into the changing of the times.

22

Change came swiftly on wings of night. The day before, guided by a mystifying impulse, her father had completed the removal of his magic books and his precious library to an unknown location. He spoke of having hidden his library deep underground. Not one of his magic books remained in the house.

He had sent away the last of the writers to an undisclosed location, with directions to last well into the remote future. There was nothing of value left in the house. The holographic exhibition of the lost masterworks, still in its development stages, but with its detailed plan fully outlined, was hidden in the basement.

That day Ruslana's father told her that he had done all that needed to be done. Rich cables to the future had been laid. All manner of designs in time had been prepared. The future was already made. It had been conjured, dreamt, made real. All that was required now was time. There was nothing more for him to do. He had set marvellous things in motion.

'Now I must become the pelican who feeds the young with its own blood.'

Not for the first time, she was perplexed by her father's riddling words. But he was not downcast. In fact, he shone, in a joyful illumination. He seemed to be sitting in a pool of brilliant light. She could not see the source of the light. For one whose talk seemed fatalistic, he was remarkably luminous. He was, it seemed, happy.

'The underground will find you at the right time, in its own surprising way. You will be a warrior of truth. You will wage war, not with violence, but with wisdom.'

He looked keenly into her eyes.

'Be a sign of what is to come,' he said. 'Trust your light. Even in failure, even in despair, even when you see the world crumbling and falling apart all around you. Even when the world seems to be at an end. Trust your light.'

He smiled.

'There are many ways to reach me.'

At that moment a tender piece of music, an almost spiritual aria, started up in a distant depth of the house. Ruslana was used to this. All through her childhood, all through the house, wherever they stayed, music was always starting up of its own accord. Her father once explained to her that the universe was full of unheard music that, with a thought, an act of will, can be heard anywhere.

She listened to the distant aria now in her father's silence. He was preparing to say something significant and she could sense it. For him silences were small initiations. He always prefaced something unique with an inflected silence. It was as though information was given first in silence and then in speech. Silence amplified speech.

Ruslana waited patiently. She prepared a place in herself for what she was about to hear. She emptied herself of thought and in vacancy waited.

23

'My time in the world of shadows is finished,' her father said. 'My time here is done. The long dream is over. The foundation is laid. Someone else is coming for the next phase. I was meant to prepare the way. But the hardest part, the time of the great war, the mighty clash, belongs to someone else. Someone special. Maybe you have glimpsed his face.'

Ruslana shivered. It was as though someone had touched the nape of her neck with a flower.

'The Hierarchy will destroy the world before they surrender. In a sense they will be right. They made the world as it is. It is fitting that they should be the ones to destroy it. But the moment it is destroyed it will be rebuilt again with a new material, made of dew. Then the world will be a book that each person writes. Each person will have their own light, and all the lights will be one.'

He paused again, his smile more brilliant now.

'As I speak to you they are at the door. Any second the bell will ring. They will come for me and I will not resist. They will take me to a dark place and they will torture me and I will smile. They will use on me whips, razors, waterdrips, and electronic prods. Then at a moment of my choosing I will step out of my body and vacate this temple of flesh and bones. I will leave my torturers with a hollow shell. I will step into the next stage of my journey. What can they do with an inert body which the occupant has vacated? They will be angry, they will beat up a corpse, and then they will throw it away.'

At that moment there was a knock at the door.

'The corpse will decompose and return to the atoms and energies in the air and the soil.'

There was the rude clamour of the doorbell.

'Maybe they will burn the corpse and their victory will turn to ashes.'

Ruslana listened as they broke down the door. Then darkness came swooping into the house.

BOOK FOUR

1

Karnak was convinced he was living not in a dream but in a nightmare. The nightmare was not the world's, but his own. He remained convinced of this as he wandered about, haunted by the face he had glimpsed once in a crowd, the face of Amalantis, his lover. He began to think he should seek medical help. He might even have done something drastic to himself if he had not witnessed something odd one day that made him think that maybe the nightmare was not his own but the world's.

He had gone to the outskirts of the city. There was a hill that he liked climbing as a child. He liked getting to the top and looking out over the city. He had gone there now on an impulse, for some quiet, to escape his restless imaginings.

He sat on the summit and gazed absent-mindedly over the world. A short distance away he noticed a tall crane on a gigantic building site. While he watched, a man in a suit and hat with a walking stick began to climb up the crane. When he got to the top he walked along the metal arm till he came to the edge. Then as if setting out on a stroll, he stepped off the edge and smashed onto the ground far below.

Karnak started screaming but no one heard. He could not believe what he had seen. Out of nowhere people converged at the place where the man had fallen. A van came and the police tumbled out and broke up the crowd.

On another day Karnak was in a park, under a tree, when he saw a woman jump from the fourth floor of a building. On another evening, in a bar, he overheard a conversation about a man who had walked off a cliff.

He gradually became aware that everywhere people were electing to walk out of life. This phenomenon was new. These were prosperous people, successful in their jobs in the city. They were perfectly normal and healthy.

The cases grew in number. During this time the wailing had continued at night. The condition of spontaneous weeping hadn't diminished either. But added to these now were the cases of perfectly normal people, with apparently happy families, electing calmly to walk out of life. It was an affront to the Hierarchy and to the myth it propagated of the world as a steady progression to the universal garden.

Sometimes she really worried him. There was that time when she took him on a long walk to one of the local psychiatric wards. They were called Houses of Renormalisation. She led him to one of its outer walls.

'Listen,' she said.

He listened, but heard nothing.

'Listen harder,' she said, 'as if you were listening to your heart.'

He listened harder and then, faintly at first, he began to hear this poignant singing. It was so gentle that he thought he was inventing it.

'Do you hear it?'

'Yes. What is it?'

'Listen again.'

He listened not harder this time, but gentler. Then he heard these voices. It was as if they were talking to the wall. Then he heard stories, rumours, hints of disasters, warnings about falling asleep, reminders to wash out one's heart, whispers about how every day the world was dying. The voices troubled him. He did not want to hear what they were saying. He pulled away.

'Who are they?' he asked.

'They are the mad. They are the sanest people in the land. They pass on secrets.'

'What kind of secrets?'

'Secrets that will bring the world to an end.'

'Let's go,' he said.

They walked away. He walked hurriedly. He wanted to be as far away from that wall as possible.

'Why did you take me there? Now I won't be able to sleep well at night.'

'Do you sleep well at night?'

'No, but now I'll sleep worse.'

'Worse is better,' was all she said, then lapsed into a silence that lasted the walk home.

2

Around that time, Karnak was standing at his window when he caught a glimpse of a word flashing across the sky. He hurried outside to get a better view. When he got down to the street he found that quite a crowd had gathered.

They were all looking up, as if expecting an invasion from the sky, or the transfiguration of the heavens. There was wonder on their upturned faces.

Karnak asked what was happening. No one answered. They just gazed at the sky. There were thick clouds above, not rain clouds, but massed clouds, like a journey of fugitive monsters. However it was not the sense of threat that showed on the gathered faces. It was the beginnings of astonishment.

It occurred to Karnak that they were awaiting a miraculous event.

3

It wasn't long before plain white vans came down the street and uniformed men scattered the crowd. The people left without complaint. They melted back to their houses, with backward glances at the sky. Soon the street was empty. But before he left, Karnak could see faces pressed against windows, looking for some promised sign in the sky.

All evening long, way into the night, they watched. The brooding clouds massed and gathered, and thin streaks of lightning tentatively rent the sky. Great rumblings sounded in unimaginable distances.

That night the wailings were more ferocious than ever.

4

The next day the clouds had cleared. The sky was grey and neutral with no threat of turbulence. People went about their business, making no references to the spontaneous gatherings or to the hopeful staring at the sky.

That day Karnak had heard two people talking behind an oak tree, and learnt that there had been spontaneous gatherings across the land. At that exact moment the day before, as if they'd felt a collective twinge, people had gone out of their houses and looked heavenward. This happened in towns and villages and big cities. Wherever there had been collective gatherings the authorities had sent in uniformed men. But today it was as if everyone had forgotten. Something had wiped out the memory of universal hope.

Karnak was so struck by what he heard, that he wanted to see who was talking. The information hadn't been in the newspapers or in the other media of rumours. It occurred to Karnak that the talkers might be connected to the question-askers in some way.

Unable to resist, he went round the tree to look. To his horror he found not two unusual-looking men, but two boys. They laughed when they saw him and went off running and laughing across the field till they became shadows.

5

One week later Karnak saw in his mind the word he had glimpsed in the sky. It came to him as he was waking from a short sleep.

When the word flashed into his mind, Karnak leapt out of bed. He had an irresistible urge to do something. He felt he should do something. Having no idea what that something was he got dressed and went out. He walked the streets aimlessly.

The word he had seen flared inside him and gave him no rest. It filled him with wild energy. It crammed him with odd ideas and inspirations. He felt that he was ready to be a warrior. He longed for conflict. He craved some great act of self-immolation, to throw himself into the flames of revolution, of adventure, of change. It was an overwhelming feeling.

He had no idea what to do with the energy that had surged in him with the seeing of the word.

He went on wandering mindlessly till he found himself in front of a blue house with a crooked gate.

He had no idea what he was doing there.

Then he snapped out of his self-absorption and realised with a shock where he was.

He was standing outside the home of his missing lover, Amalantis.

6

It was as if he'd woken from a dream. Unable to move, he stared at the blue house till tears welled up in his eyes. He had no idea how he had arrived at the house that held so many sad and beautiful memories.

He was about to turn and flee from the pain when he heard a grating noise. A woman stuck her head out of a first storey window and cried in a bold voice:

'You there, what in the bloody hell are you looking at?'

Karnak started.

'Are you a thief or a spy or what?'

Karnak was embarrassed and began hurrying away. Then the voice changed.

'Stop! I know you!'

Without knowing why, he began to run.

'Stop that man! Stop him! Yes, that man, stop him!' the woman cried, raising the alarm in the neighbourhood.

Karnak bounded down the street and a group of men near a lorry chased after him. Acutely aware of the absurdity of being pursued like a common criminal, he ran as fast as he could. Panic filled his chest. As he was turning a corner, one of the men brought him down with a flying tackle. Many bodies bundled on top of him. He was pinned to the ground, his head bruised, his back scuffed, elbows and knees on his chest. He tried to shout but couldn't. Then he faded into darkness.

When he opened his eyes again he saw the mother of Amalantis. She was staring down at him with unsympathetic eyes. One of the men helped him up.

'Where did you think you were going?' the man said, giving him a comradely thump on the back.

'Okay, boys, I've got him,' the mother said. 'Back to your business. Thanks for your help.'

The men faded back to their lorry. Locking him with a firm grip at the elbow, she led Karnak back to the house. She opened the front gate and shut it with a backward kick.

7

Karnak found himself in the living room. It was still very familiar to him. He had spent many hours in the same chair he was in now. He would sit, listening to the clock tick on the wall. Amalantis would be seated across from him, watching him with a playful smile. He hadn't been there in a long time.

The mother subjected Karnak to the long scrutiny of a friendly witch. She had always regarded him with suspicion. The silence between them, amplified by the ticking of the big clock on the wall, continued for a long while. Karnak fell into a white hole in his mind. After staring blankly at him the mother spoke:

'Why has it taken you so long to come and see me?'

Karnak woke from his trance and saw the picture of Amalantis on the wall opposite. It was a picture of dewy loveliness. She was gazing at him with her unique and mysterious smile. He never understood her smile.

'My world has collapsed,' he said, 'and I don't know who I am any more.'

She gave him a look of cutting irony.

'You have no idea what I have been through,' she said, without pity.

'I dread to imagine. It's been terrible for me and you're her mother.'

She stared at him as though he were speaking a foreign language.

'What did you know about my daughter?'

'I loved her like life itself. To me she was like the sun in the heavens. I am in darkness without her.'

The mother stared at him as if he had acquired tentacles. She considered him for a long time.

'This daughter of mine whom you claim to love like the sun is not who you think she is.'

Her words had a startling effect on him. He felt something dark pass across his eyes. He struggled against unconsciousness. As he flailed in the tomb of his mind, he heard her continue.

'She was born strange. She is not a child of this earth. All her life she was never where she ought to be. One day when she was two and a half she began speaking a language no one had ever heard before. Her body was not like anyone else's. When she cut herself, you blinked and it was healed. She was always telling us about things before they happened. She saw everything we did in her dreams. When she was eight she told us that someone we knew was going to die soon, and the person died. When she was five, one morning at breakfast, she told us that we were all living in prison. This scared the hell out of her father. I broke down and began crying. She just stared at us with those beautiful clear eyes of hers. Almost in pity.'

The mother paused and moved towards the window and sat on the sill, half-turned away from Karnak.

'She said that many times. When we were eating, when she was playing, even when she was going to bed. "You're all in prison. Can't you see it?" she'd say sweetly, with her pretty face looking at you intently. We thought she'd grow out of it, but she got worse. "You're all going to go mad. Can't you see it?" she would say. Then a bit later, she would say: "You're all asleep. Can't you see it?" She was a trial to us. She would say these things to us, with the loveliest smile. We began to think there was something not right about her. "You all think there's something not quite right about me, don't you?" she'd say. "But you're all wrong. I'm fine, but you're all deceived."

'"Who's deceiving us, honey?" I'd ask her.

'"Everything," she'd say.

'"What do you mean?" I'd ask.

'"The Hierarchy," she'd say.

'"Don't say such things," I would say, hushing her up.

'She was about eight or nine. Then one morning she said:

'"One day you'll all be wailing in your sleep."

'"Why, honey?" I said.

'"Because you all deny so much."

'"What do we deny, honey?" I asked.

'"The wickedness and the suffering," she said, as if she were reciting a nursery rhyme.

'Then one day, when she was ten, she said:

'"I'll be taken away one afternoon, and then your troubles will begin."

'Not long after that she disappeared. We were distraught.

This strange child was the love of our lives. She was gone for forty days. And then one lovely spring morning, with the flowers opening, there she was, playing in the middle of the garden, as if she'd never been away. She wouldn't tell us where she'd been or what had happened to her. When she came back she wasn't our lovely little daughter any more. She grew silent. She stopped saying strange things. She began to do things that alarmed us and could have got us into trouble. She began bringing books into the house.'

'Books?' Karnak cried.

'Yes, books. No one in the house had seen books for generations. We didn't even know what they were. We'd only heard that they were poisonous and that they ruined the mind, and that no one was to have anything to do with them. We saw her with these strange objects and we asked what they were and she said:

"Books."

"What are they?" we asked.

'And she said:

"They keep things."

"What's wrong with a good old suitcase?" I said.

"They reveal things."

"Like what?"

"Like what you are."

"How do they do that?" I asked.

"They're like a mirror," she said. "You look into them and you see yourself."

'"Let me see that," I said, and took the object from her. It opened and I stared at it and I saw these funny things in it. They seemed to be moving, but they were still. Then as I looked I saw something that frightened me. I'm not sure what it was, but it gave my heart a jump. I could have sworn I caught a glimpse of the Devil. I dropped it and it screamed when it hit the ground as if it were a living thing. I ran away in horror.'

She stopped speaking for a moment and wiped her face. Karnak wasn't sure if they were tears.

'After that we kept our eyes on her. She spent hours huddled over those things. She'd be silent. How can anyone sit in silence staring at a piece of wood for so long? Sometimes she'd laugh. Then she would shut the object and stare straight ahead. Then a few days later she would say something. She'd say things that didn't make sense.

'"Find the original myth," she would say. She'd say it under her breath. She'd say it not to herself, but to us, as if she wanted us to hear. After that, she began disappearing. Sometimes for a week. When she returned she always looked more beautiful and more strange. Sometimes I'd see her in the garden, just sitting and listening. What was she listening to? I could never hear.

'"What are you listening to?" I'd ask.

'She'd be still as if she were dead. Quiet as a butterfly she'd say:

'"I'm listening to the stories in the air," or "I'm listening to what's going to happen," or "I'm listening to the ants in the grass."

'Now what kind of person talks like that? She frightened me. One day she said:

'"Can you hear it?"

'"Can I hear what?" I said back.

'"The music of the stars," she said, pointing a finger skyward.

'I didn't know what to do, whether to fall at her feet and worship her, or call the authorities and have her taken away for treatment. She always said those strange things with a smile that grew sweeter as she grew older. That's another thing about her. She grew older but she never seemed to change. She was like some weird flower, always as fresh as dawn. But her eyes worried me. They were innocent and kind but she looked at people with such pity, as if an axe hung over their heads that only she could see. It used to drive me mad the way she looked at people, the way she looked at me. One day I told her about it and this hurt expression appeared on her face that made me cry. I don't know why I did that. But she put her arms around me and whispered something into my ear. But I didn't hear what she said till much later, when she'd gone out for a walk. Do you know what she said?'

8

The way she asked the question startled Karnak out of his mesmerism. He was stunned to be addressed so directly. He shook his head.

The mother studied him as if he had just woken from an inappropriate doze.

'Why should I tell you? You're not even listening.'

'I am listening, with all my being,' Karnak said awkwardly.

The mother made a ferocious but tender gesture with her hand, then she continued:

'She said: "I'm in your heart like a butterfly." Now what does that mean? I thought about it all day. Then I realised I must have got it wrong and she'd said:

'"You're in my heart like a butterfly."

'This moved me, but I don't know why. She went away then and only came back three days later. She said she was working now. She had a job, at last.

'"What work are you doing?" we asked.

'"Good work. The best work," she said.

'"Are you being paid?" we asked.

'"Paid for ever and ever," she said.

'What does that mean? Her disappearances increased. We got worried. We searched her room one day and found notes that we couldn't read. We found those strange objects called books. We found a drawing. It was a drawing of us looking through her things. She had known we would do it. She even knew the day we would do it. We left her room in a hurry, as if we were chased by dogs.'

The mother opened a window, stuck her head out, and shouted something at the men clustered round the lorry. After a minute they got into the lorry and drove away. She shut the window. She appeared distracted for a moment, then she went on:

'She seemed to have lots of friends. But we never saw them. She seemed to travel a lot, all over the world. But we didn't know how she did it. She seemed to know things that were going on that no one heard about, things that were not even on the radio. Things not in the papers. Sometimes up in her room we'd hear several voices. They'd be voices we'd never heard before. But when we went up, there was only her in the room. Even the window would be shut.'

The mother paused long enough to send a shiver of a look at Karnak.

'Then to our great surprise you turn up at the house one day. Her first boyfriend. We never even knew she thought about things like that. You came here, you sat in silence, and she went on getting stranger and stranger, and you never even noticed.'

She snorted mildly.

'One day the authorities showed up and began to watch the house. At first I didn't think it was us they were watching. Why would anyone watch us? We're normal people. Normal decent hard-working people. We thought they were watching the people next door. Then someone came to the house and asked about our daughter.

'"What's she done?" we asked.

'"Nothing," they said. "Do you know where she goes, what she does?"

'"No," we replied.

'"Do you know whether she is part of any dangerous groups trying to destabilise society?"

'"No," we laughed. "Not our daughter."

'"Do you know if she is part of any groups trying to overthrow the Hierarchy?"

'"Overthrow? No," we said. "Absolutely not. Never, never, never. Not our daughter."

'"Do you know if she is in league with any powers from another planet, another galaxy?"

'"What!" we cried. "Another planet? Are you having us on? No, no, no. Not our daughter. You've got it wrong!"

'"Thank you for your time," the man said, and then he was gone. He just disappeared. We didn't even see which way he went.'

She gave a half-smile.

'The next time I see her, Amalantis has a red rose in her hand. She gives it to me, along with a kiss. That brings tears to my eyes. What has been going on, my tears ask her. She gives me a hug and then does something strange. I wished her father were still there so he could have seen it too. Did I tell you that my husband died around that time? Well, he did. Strange circumstances. Anyway, she did something strange.'

Karnak found his voice for an instant.

'What?'

She gave him a look as if she had no intention of telling him. Then her eyes grew dim.

'She wrapped something from the air. She wrapped it in her palm. And when she opened her hand I could have sworn I saw a light. Maybe it was a word. Maybe it was a butterfly. It could have been any of them. Then she put it to my forehead. It burnt me like a white-hot kiss and I went a bit dizzy. Then she said she was going to see you, and she left.'

9

The mother's eyes brightened. She was gazing into the distance, beyond the walls of the room.

'When she left, this peculiar feeling expanded in my brain. It travelled all round my body and settled in my heart. In the middle of the night I woke up screaming, as if my heart was on fire. But it was not a bad fire. It was just that I wasn't used to it. Then it cooled and spread throughout my body. In the morning when I woke up I was different. I suddenly understood. But I don't know what I understood. Not long afterwards I learnt she had been taken away and that I might never see her again. How did I find it out? I don't know. It was as if someone told me, or as if they announced it on the radio. Then one afternoon as I sat in her favourite chair in the garden, trying to hear the ants in the grass, the doorbell sounded. There was a little boy at the door. He told me very sweetly that he had been sent to tell me that they'd taken my daughter away, but not to worry. Then he was gone, as if I had dreamt him. Ever since, it's been awful. I sit here at night listening to all the wailing I had never heard before.'

10

She paused and looked at Karnak as though there was another side of the story that she hadn't told him yet.

'Why has it taken you so long to come and see me? Especially when the suffering has been so great?'

He was about to reply, but she raised a palm of silence.

'Don't say anything. She told me many things about you which I didn't understand at the time.'

Karnak looked surprised.

'She knew you better than you know yourself. I'm ashamed to say this, but she loved you as much as a mother loves her only child.'

'She did?'

It came out of him like a sob.

'She said you appear to be one thing to the world, but deep down you are another. She said you seem gentle and silent and timid, but that in truth you are a chariot-rider, a prince. She said you're a hero who would go deep into the underworld, if necessary, to find her and change the water of the earth.'

The mother pulled a face.

'I know. She said such grandiose things. But she was often right. She said you would be lost for a long time and people would think you had gone mad, but that you would be the first to start to see how things really are. She said your greatest strength is love and when all the towers are tumbling down and everyone is losing it that your star will still be shining. And now here you are. If you hadn't come to see me I couldn't have told you all this now, could I?'

Karnak was moved.

'No,' he replied meekly.

Then after a moment's thought:

'When did she tell you all these things?'

'Mostly when I expressed doubts about you. But I only heard them later, in bits and pieces. That's how she is. She comes back to you, later, long afterwards, when you are thinking of something else.'

'She has not come back to me yet,' Karnak said sadly.

'She will. But you've got to let her. That's what has helped my grief. I let her come back to me in her own way.'

Karnak looked at the mother with a new understanding.

'There is more you want to tell me, isn't there?' he said.

'A lot more,' she said with a sigh and a smile. 'But not now. There's only so much the ears can hear.'

11

They sat for a long time in silence in the living room. The picture of Amalantis stared at him all that time, her stare full of kindness, devoid of reproach. Her smile was wistful and loving.

He sat there in the gathering darkness. She let the dark close around them. Then the clock struck a strange hour, and Karnak leapt up as if bitten.

'I've taken up too much of your time. I must be going. Thank you for…'

'Don't thank me for anything. I know what you're going through. I see what's happening. My daughter's disappearance taught me to see.'

She stood up.

'Be careful now,' she said.

Then she left him standing there in the middle of the room and disappeared into the darkness of the house.

Karnak waited. He heard nothing. He waited some more. Then he realised that in her own way she had already said goodbye.

One day Amalantis came back with all these seeds. She was quietly excited. She held them in the palm of her hand as if they were magic seeds.

'What are they?'

'Seeds.'

'I know they're seeds. What are you going to do with them?'

'Plant them.'

'No one plants things. No one is allowed to plant things. Do you have permission?'

'I'm going to plant them and watch them grow.'

'What if they find out?'

'They won't find out.'

'Where will you plant them?'

'In my room.'

A few weeks later she took him to a cupboard and opened it. He saw these bright roses growing from a pot. He had never seen anything grow before. They were both beautiful and scary. He wanted to run from them, but he was also drawn by their strange unfamiliar beauty.

'Smell them.'

'No.'

'Why not?'

'Seeing them is bad enough.'

'Is it so bad to see them?'

'I didn't mean that.'

'I know.'

'I'll smell them another time. Let me get used to just seeing them.'

BOOK FIVE

1

On a beautiful day in the middle of the year a rumour rose from the underworld. It began a feverish journey from mouth to ear across the land. At first the rumour seemed improbable. But its improbability lent it fascination. Its unlikeliness accelerated the speed of its progress.

Soon fragments of the rumour reached the sleeping world. Some claimed they dreamt it. Some said they had heard it on the radio. Some said a drunk had whispered it to them. The fragments grew. Each fragment was a full-fledged story.

Then the fragments warred with one another. A fragment of rumour said that a flash of lightning had one night struck the great tower of the Hierarchy. The luminous crown on its summit, which shone a dark light on the world, had come tumbling down. Another fragment claimed that the tower had burst into flames in five places. Another fragment maintained that members of the Hierarchy were seen falling upside down from the tower. There were no official reports of any such things. No deaths of Hierarchy members were ever broadcast.

In a separate fragment of the same rumour, a boy was seen walking in the air. He walked from the summit of the highest hill in the city. He was dressed like a fool. He had his head thrown back in a carefree way. There was a mysterious knapsack with an open eye on a stick over his shoulder. He walked over the precipice and walked in the air and the dogs on the ground below barked excitedly at this new arrival to the city. The rumour of this arrival was so persistent and widespread that the authorities, alarmed by intimations of a miracle, closed off the hill where the boy was supposed to have walked in the air.

In yet another fragment of the rumour a boy driving a chariot was seen careering down the high street. The chariot was pulled by two sphinxes, one black, the other white. People had seen it and not believed what they saw. They forgot about it till later that day when rumours circulated the city. Some said the boy had a pentagram on his forehead. Some said there were stars on the canopy of the chariot. Others claimed that the boy who rode the chariot was a king and he controlled the two sphinxes with invisible reins.

Some spoke with awe of the sublime determined look on the handsome face of the boy-king. Not long afterwards the police swarmed the high street and scattered the crowds.

It was a time when rumours and fragments of rumours filled the world. These were not rumours about the end of time. These were rumours of disaster. Fires were said to have broken out in the great tower of the Hierarchy. The fallen crown on its summit had not been replaced. It was said that the Hierarchy didn't know how to replace it. The architects who could reconstruct it had disappeared and the builders were in the mental asylums. Dense smoke hung over the tower. No one could locate the source of the fires.

These were rumours but people were not inclined to believe them. To the general mind the Hierarchy was all-powerful and all-seeing. The Hierarchy was eternal.

But for the first time in generations, like bats flitting at night, there were doubts in the secret chambers of the general mind.

2

Rumours and fragments of rumours proliferated. There was talk of a woman in a field who opened a lion's mouth with the lightest touch. She was a slender woman in a dazzling white shift, with roses in her hair. There were roses in a ringlet round the neck of the lion.

The rumours spoke with awe of the way, with a touch, the woman had opened the lion's mouth. On successive nights people said that in their dreams they had heard the lion roar.

Some said the roar shook the foundations of the tower.

Around that time people said they saw the Devil. Some said they saw him on a dark night. The Devil had the head of a goat, the body of a man, the breasts of a woman, and the claws of an eagle. It had two horizontal horns, the ears of an ass, and the giant wings of a bat. Some said there was an inverted pentagram on its forehead and that it was perched on a split slab of cubic stone.

Some rumours said that two members of the Hierarchy were chained by the neck to the cracked cubic stone. One was a man, the other a woman, and they were both naked. Fragments of the rumour said the Devil held a flaming torch in its left hand and that the Hierarchy members had long tails.

These were rumours swirling from the underworld. The

rumours infected the world where people sleep and scream, where they live and wail. The rumours took wing like bats at night.

3

No one knew where the tower of the Hierarchy was. No one had seen the tower. It was only when the rumours began to circulate that anyone heard of the existence of the tower. They had no idea that the Hierarchy had anything to do with a tower.

But the tower standing on the peak of a lonely rock grew in the minds of the populace. Rumour said the tower was twenty-two storeys high. Other rumours said that it was merely composed of twenty-two layers of brick. All the rumours agreed that it had three windows. All the rumours also agreed that, due to an unusual atmospheric condition, it was always pitch black around the tower.

4

The most persistent rumour of all was of the arrival in the city of a strange boy. Some said they had seen him descend from the sky in a spacecraft. Others said they had seen a star fall from the sky and found this innocent boy with uncanny eyes where the star had fallen.

But the most probable of the rumours held that one day a boy dressed like a fool in a garment stitched with eight-pointed stars had arrived in the city. He had a dog at his heel and a knapsack with an open eye on his back. He caused havoc wherever he went. The nature of the havoc caused was never made clear.

Some said he caused havoc in the hearts of women. It was said that women who gazed on him fell in love with him instantly. Wherever he went people burst into joyful song. Some said his presence induced visions. There was much talk of spontaneous healing.

Strange rumours held that trees blossomed at his passing and flowers grew out of the ground on which he had trod. It was said he could appear and disappear at will. He was seen in several places at the same time.

People became curious and crowds gathered.

'Have you seen him? Have you seen him?' they cried.

They would rush to the nearest park. Then he was seen on a hill. The sick and diseased and troubled of mind hurried to that hill. It turned out that everyone was sick in mind. All were weighed down with fears and troubles. All were full of despair.

People abandoned their work. Doctors and patients, bankers and clients, mothers and children, teachers and students went in great waves to behold this strange boy who had come to the city on whispers of glory.

When they finally got to the hilltop they found not a boy dressed as a fool, but a boy dressed as a magician. He had a wand pointing upward and a finger pointing to the depths of the earth. Some believed he was pointing to the underworld.

He was surrounded by trees with ripe fruit, trees in flower. Before him were flowering bushes of lilies and roses. Near him was a table. On the table was a wand, a chalice, a sword, and a golden coin with the sign of a pentagram.

He wore a red cloak. There was a wreath on his head and above him some discerned the mysterious sign of eternity. He was heard reciting fragments of the original myth.

They beheld him in stillness.

When he finished his recitation there was a sudden flash of light in the sky. Some people heard in the silence that followed the ominous but magical sound of a tolling bell. Then in a heartbeat the boy was gone.

The sick who were present said they had been spontaneously cured. Many who were blind found that they could see. Their cries of jubilation caused panic in the crowds.

5

The strange boy was next seen by the river.

Beyond the river people lived in fear and did not know it. Beyond the river was the centre of the city. It was like a fortress, with walled houses and giant watchtowers. The wailing at night had encroached far into the daytime. At dawn as people went to work in their suits and formal dresses it was not unknown for one of them to break down. One afternoon a man was seen with a gun. He was shouting and shooting into the crowd. When he was finally grappled to the ground it was discovered that he was fast asleep.

One morning a woman in the crowd was on her way to work when she suddenly tore off her clothes and ran through the streets singing holy songs long forgotten by the people.

A week later another woman did the same thing. She stripped naked and ran through the streets singing. But that day changed the history of the world. For the police chased after the woman, caught up with her and, in full public view, ate her raw. They tore her flesh and drank her blood and ate chunks of her buttocks and gorged themselves on her bones.

After that a new madness came among the people.

At night, in a restless neighbourhood, someone might be heard screaming. Those who looked out of the window saw a white van appear outside the house. An hour later men in uniforms would be seen emerging from the house with blood on their faces and blood and gristle on their shirts as if they had been feasting on raw wild animals. The next day nothing but the cracked skull and the long bones of the victim were seen in the bedroom.

A new stage in the elimination of undesirables had been reached.

6

No longer were those who transgressed dragged away to unknown places. No longer were they thrown in grinding machines. The Hierarchy, in its wisdom, unleashed a new form of punishment. All those who were not contributing to the happiness of society, all those who sought to undermine the state, to undermine the new myths, all these people would be eaten. They would be devoured by a special police force.

Those who saw them at night said they had the faces of wild dogs. The old said they had the faces of jackals. But when members of this special police force were seen in daylight they had handsome faces with strong jaws. They seemed healthy young men and women in their prime.

7

It was around this time, when whole sections of the populace were being eaten by the state jackals, that the strange boy was seen by the river. The cry of his sighting went from mouth to mouth. Great numbers flocked to catch a glimpse of him.

He wore a cuirass and golden-blue armour. He looked like a warrior-king. He came down from his star-spangled chariot and stood there before the gathered people and gazed upon them in silence.

They were fascinated by his chariot. No one had seen such a thing before. Some saw hints of an infinite sky on the canopy of the chariot. Others were amazed at the two sphinxes that pulled it. They stood perfectly still.

The gathered people looked at the boy-warrior in vague expectation. Was he going to speak to them? There were many who were sick in the crowd; many lame, who had been carried; many blind, who had been led; many crawling with diseases, who had been borne on litters. Those who seemed whole were riddled with neuroses, with discontent, insomnia, rage, misery, fear, and great sicknesses of the spirit.

There were some among them who were rich beyond description and spent their days going from guru to oracle, seeking cures for mysterious perennial illnesses. There were some who were very famous and who were among the unhappiest people in the land.

Many of the rich and famous were devourers of others. In their sleep they turned into jackal-faces and devoured their neighbours. They ate their neighbours in their sleep and didn't know it. They were known to howl at night like blinded bulls.

Many of the devourers were lords and baronesses and knights. They were the pillars of society, the doughty men and women of the realm. Many of them were in the crowd. There were also many children in the crowd, devourers in training, with sweet innocent faces, carried on the shoulders of their devourer parents.

The judges and doctors, the ministers of state and the directors of broadcasting stations, the ordinary citizens, all stood and watched the boy-warrior. They watched to see what he would do, what miracles he would perform.

But the boy-warrior gazed back at them. His golden-blue armour flashed dazzling lights into their eyes. He seemed intent only on studying them. And when he had studied them enough he stepped back into his chariot. With a crack of the invisible reins, he drove right through the crowd, and vanished into a vision.

There were cries of bafflement. One moment there, the next gone. Many in the crowd who could see were blinded.

He could never explain her disappearances. She was always disappearing. When she came back she always had an amazing light around her. She always looked unusually healthy and well. Always glowing.

'Where do you go?'

'Nowhere.'

'Where is nowhere?'

'Nowhere.'

'Is there someone else?'

'Never.'

'Is there someone else?'

'That can never be.'

'Is there someone else?'

'You've got the key to my body and my heart.'

'Why don't you tell me where you go?'

'It's best if you don't know.'

'But why? Don't you trust me?'

'I trust you with my life, that's why.'

'You speak in riddles. I don't understand.'

'There's nothing to understand.'

'Where do you go?'

'Nowhere.'

'Nowhere?'

'Nowhere.'

'Why are you so different when you come back?'

'Am I?'

'You come back with a glow.'

'Do I?'

'Does nowhere give you this glow?'

'It must do then.'

'Can I come with you the next time?'

Amalantis would go off again, into that deep world of thought, with that curious smile in her eyes.

8

They used to be afraid of the darkness and the disappearances. Now they were afraid of being devoured. It was not unknown for people to be eaten in their sleep. It was not unknown to be eaten on a visit to the bank. Political rallies became notorious places for being suddenly devoured.

The consumption of people was confined initially to the jackal-headed figures of the night who emerged from white vans. Now the activity had spread. Normal people next to you at a concert might suddenly sprout a jackal-face and bite off a chunk of your shoulder. Famous artists became devourers overnight. A party, a dance, or a dinner, among friends, became occasions for the hosts to turn on their guests and devour them. It was increasingly common for guests to pounce on their hosts and eat them for dinner. They could often be seen leaving with contented expressions on their bloodied faces.

It got so bad that children were devoured at school, in their classrooms, by other children. Sometimes they were eaten by their teachers. Sometimes they ate their teachers alive.

People were not always devoured whole. They often had large chunks bitten out of them. It was not unusual to see someone who was whole one day and armless the next. They might even be without a leg. They might have a side of their face bitten off as if by a giant dog.

These maimings and devourings were not reported in the papers. But it became a source of pride to be known as a devourer. The devourers became the most respected, most feared, most celebrated people of the times.

The real shame was to be among the devoured. It was thought better to be dead than to wander about the world with the badge of your devouring, a missing arm, a hollow chest, a bitten off nose.

9

As the devouring of people got worse, so did the rumours from the underworld. It was said that a woman dressed like an angel was seen pouring water from golden vessels onto the head of a lion and the head of an eagle. This took place on the shore of the river. The woman had one foot on earth and the other in the water. No one knew what to make of such an elaborate rumour.

The effect of all these rumours, all these sightings, was to awaken unrest in the populace. The Hierarchy responded by putting out instructions that the boy-warrior be arrested at the first opportunity. Police officers and soldiers were deployed across the land. In this way a universal state of emergency was imposed. Sirens sounded everywhere.

Then one evening the boy-warrior was seen in a park, under a ghostly light. This sighting was the strangest. He was first seen by a child. Reports of the sighting flew round the city and people abandoned their jobs and left their homes and schools and poured to the field where the boy-warrior was said to be. They came and saw something they did not understand. They saw a boy hanging upside down from a beam. He was a little grown now. He was hanging from a rope attached to his right foot. His left foot was crossed behind his right foot at an angle, as if he had stopped in the middle of a country dance. He was upside down and his arms were folded in front of him. His rich hair, white and luminous, pointed straight down towards the earth. There was a soft light about his head, and an expression of sublime tranquillity on his face. His eyes were smiling. It was as if upside down was the best way to be, the right way to see things.

The sighting of the boy-warrior hanging upside down perplexed the gathered crowd. They didn't know what to do. They just stood there and stared at him as if he were a sign, a new language that they had to learn.

They stared in silence. He stared back peacefully. When the authorities learnt about this new appearance of the boy-warrior, troops were sent to the field in great numbers. White vans surrounded the area. Armed police splintered the crowd with violence, causing great commotion. But when they closed in on the boy-warrior hanging upside down from a cross-beam, they were struck by his stillness. He was perfectly still and serene, like a pendulum that had come to a stop.

For a moment the armed police hesitated. Then their senior officer barked out an order and they woke from their mesmerism. They rushed at the hanging boy, but when they got to the beam they found he wasn't there. Only the rope was left dangling. They arrested the rope as necessary evidence.

10

Feeling itself undermined by the escapades of the boy-warrior, and weakened by the persistent rumours flowing from the underworld, the Hierarchy unleashed a regime of unprecedented ferocity on the populace.

People were not allowed to gather in certain places. There were more arrests. There was an epidemic of devouring. People disappeared at alarming rates. Whenever people congregated somewhere the police would descend and scatter them. People were spied on in the streets, at work, and in their homes.

During this period there was a silence of signs. No words sprouted on billboards, or on roads, or on the sides of lorries. No words were stencilled on walls or appeared in the sky. It seemed a victory had been wrought over the question-askers.

The truth is that there was a new silence in the land. The people who went to work in the morning had faces that were bleak and dissatisfied. If they were still asleep then it was a bad and bitter sleep.

The victory of the Hierarchy seemed complete in the apparent silence of the land. But from the underworld rumours bubbled up, quietly poisoning the silence.

11

Fragments of rumour had it that a high priestess, with a blue mantle over her white garment, wearing a strange crown, sat between two pillars on a high hill. One pillar was black, the other was white. She had a scroll in her right hand. The scroll was partially visible. On it could be discerned a strange incomplete word. Some said the word was Taro or Tora or The La or Revea or Apocal. Rumour also had it that there was a bower of flowers behind her. She wore a white cross round her neck.

There were other rumours that spoke of an empress seated in a rich field of wheat, by a flowing river. All around her was abundance. She had yellow hair, wore a crown of twelve stars on her head, had a sceptre in her hand, and a crescent moon beneath her feet. She was a gateway to a magic scene of nature. No one knew what to make of these rumours. They were received in silence, and passed on in whispers.

12

In those dark times, when all had given up hope of catching a glimpse of him, the boy-warrior was seen again. He was seen in the cameo of Justice, holding aloft a sapphire sword, seated between two pillars, with a green crown on his head. Children saw him on their way from school.

This time, before great crowds could gather, the authorities heard about it, and swiftly surrounded the area. It was in full view of the converging populace that he was arrested. The boy-warrior was borne on his throne to the back of a white van. To everyone's astonishment he made no attempts to resist arrest. He submitted himself to them without a fuss. Some said there was an expression of sublime calm on his face.

The gathered people, expecting a miracle, some marvellous mode of escape that had been characteristic of the boy-warrior so far, were amazed at the arrest. They watched in silence as the white van hurried away, among a convoy of military vehicles.

The rumour of the boy-warrior's arrest went swiftly round the land. That night there was an uneasy silence. Not many people slept.

13

The next day, at dawn, something new emerged from the underworld. The cities were covered not with a word as before, but with a single image. The walls and the billboards and the roads and the sides of lorries were covered with this single image. It was the image of a woman in prison, of a man behind bars. A faint light shone from behind the figure in prison. This mute image descended on people as they staggered to work after a sleepless night. Papers with the image of the person imprisoned fell like grim confetti from the sky. It papered the streets and landed on the heads of commuters and city-dwellers.

At first the populace did not notice this cascade of the image on them. Like fat rough snow, the image fell on them and they did not notice. They were practically sleepless. Then at a crossing, waiting for the light to change, a young woman looked at the image on a paper and gave out a cry of recognition.

The cry communicated something to those around her. Slowly they picked up the fallen bills and looked at the image and a collective gasp of recognition flowed through the streets. Gasps turned to murmurs. Murmurs turned to speech. Speech turned to shouts. Then an unnamed commotion began in the heart of the sleepwalking world.

14

It was a commotion without a purpose. Here and there people were shouting. There was talk of rioting. No one knew how to riot. No one had done it in recorded time. People stood around, arrested by an emotion they did not know how to express. This unfocused rage left the sleepwalking city dazed, and uneasily aware of its own condition.

What was it that had so stirred them? What was it in the image of the prisoner that had broken through their sleepwalking?

The cries from the crossroads, from the streets, the howls at bus stops, the sudden breakdowns of drivers, commuters, workers, managers, and road-sweeps hinted that perhaps the cry was not for something perceived in the world, but for something perceived in themselves.

People woke up on that dawn and saw their faces in a mirror in the streets. They sensed, in a flash, that they were the ones in prison. This was the conjecture put forward by those who wrote the chronicles of the times. This is not proven. Storytellers sometimes see things before they have been experienced.

15

The commotion in the cities gathered force. Barricades were set up. Groups swelled in number. An unknown voice was heard to cry:

'Not crushed like a flower.'

In the manner of Chinese whispers the phrase was passed on by wandering groups.

'Find the tower! Find the tower!'

Crowds converged, crowds swelled, the roads filled up, work was abandoned for the day. People simply stopped working and went outside and joined the huge flowing stream of voices chanting and calling out and shouting. If ever there was a crowd in search of a reason, this was it. With one voice, they sought the tower of the Hierarchy. They marched to one square and then to another. The truth is that they didn't know what they were searching for. They didn't know the focus of all their undefined anger, their numinous fears. They had caught a glimpse of themselves in prison and they sought their jailers in vain.

The truth was that no one knew where the tower of the Hierarchy was. No one had ever seen the Hierarchy and no one knew what it looked like. They sought shadows in vain. The bizarre fact was that they roamed and searched and shouted in the streets, but not a single figure of authority confronted them that day.

By the day's end the steam of their vague fury was spent. Exhausted and disappointed, they dispersed back to their homes under the gloom of night.

BOOK SIX

1

Karnak had heard all the rumours that swirled round the city. He had heard about all the sightings of the boy-warrior, but had never seen the boy-warrior himself. Every time he heard of a sighting he had rushed there, but the crowds were scattered and he arrived too late. All he got was the afterglow of the magical event as people talked about it in the heat of invention.

He did not know whether to believe what he had heard or not. He hadn't been the same since his meeting with the mother of Amalantis. He was more accepting of what he saw, no longer alarmed at seeing neighbours with a chunk of thigh missing or a face chewed off. When he saw a woman he knew with only the stump of an arm he was no longer taken aback. Something about the visit to Amalantis's house had made him accept the facts of the world. It had made him begin to see reality.

He feared that his heart had died, that some feeling for the suffering of the world had died in him too. How could he see the casual horrors without extreme distress?

One day he was looking out of his window when he saw a bejewelled car pull up at the kerb. Two men got out. He thought that they had jackal-faces but wasn't sure. While he stared he saw the two men fall upon a homeless young man from the area. They fell on him and devoured him in broad daylight. They ate him with such fury and at such speed that there wasn't even a bone or a skull to show that a human being lay there by the roadside. Their jackal-faces returned to normal faces and the two men slid back into their sparkling car and sped off.

Karnak watched this from his window as if in a dream and was so stunned by what he saw that he had to lie down. He couldn't bring himself to believe what he had seen. He fell into a traumatised sleep. Then he had a dream in which women with jackal-faces were about to devour him, and he woke up howling.

After that, a flame died in him. He kept expecting people to leap on him at any moment and devour him. He kept to himself and went out less often. Shadows and dark places quivered with jackal-faces. When he did go out he didn't speak to anyone and he noticed that the fields were empty. Children no longer played in the parks.

He noticed that the mood of the people had changed. He got the feeling that people were looking at one another out of the corner of their eyes. Even when they were not facing you they were looking at you.

He sensed that everyone feared what he feared. Everyone expected to be pounced on and eaten alive by secret jackal-faces in their midst, faces that seemed so normal. Just being spoken to made people jump in fright. When they walked down the street people seemed to walk as far away from the next person as possible.

Women ran from place to place without stopping. Old women scurried quickly away. Young men looked in every direction as they walked.

There was an acute nervousness everywhere.

2

On the day the images of the imprisoned man cascaded down, Karnak was on his way back from the Work Generation Centre. A wet bill slapped him in the face. He tore it off and looked at it. Touched by an obscure light that seemed to shine from the image itself, he experienced a moment of revelation.

He stood there staring at the image. Suddenly he felt something become clearer within him. White birds in formation flew past in the sky. They wheeled and circled and without counting he knew there were eighteen of them. For a moment they froze in the sky. Above them was the moon, which he hadn't noticed till then. In that moment the birds were like droplets of the sweating moon.

He felt the drops on his face and it occurred to him that the moon was weeping. He became aware of the road he was standing on, and saw that it ran between buildings with battlements and crenellations. The road seemed a dull yellow.

The birds scattered in the air and the moment passed. With the passing of the moment he felt as if he had been freed from a mental frame. He felt unknotted. He went home, lighter.

3

That evening while Karnak stood at the window looking at the moon, he noticed a movement among the shadows on the road below. Then he saw a girl lurking there. He stared at her for a while, wondering what she was doing there in these dangerous times.

Then as he felt himself less vacant it occurred to him that the girl was staring up at his window. Not long afterwards a car went past and its crude headlights picked her out as she tried to hide in the bushes. It took him a while to grasp what he had seen. It was the girl from the bookshop, Ruslana. He hadn't seen her for a long time, but he recognised her instantly.

He hurried downstairs and sought the girl in the street. He couldn't find her. The street was deserted. A bird nearby piped out a broken melody. He wandered far in the darkness of the street, and became a little afraid. Feeling that he must have imagined what he saw, he turned back. Near the pillar of a darkened house where the night seemed most intense, he could have sworn he saw the darkness move. He turned in the opposite direction.

He hadn't gone far when he heard a sound behind him. He swung round and saw a jackal-face staring at him. With a cry he started to run, but he heard a girl's voice.

'It's me.'

It was Ruslana, with a flower in one hand and the mask of a jackal-face in the other.

'You scared me. I could have died of fright.'

'Sorry.'

'You shouldn't scare people like that in these horrible times.'

'I really am sorry,' she said. 'But the mask protects me. Without it I could not be here.'

Karnak was still breathing heavily from fright.

'What are you doing here?' he asked, when he had recovered.

'I've come to collect you. Something is happening at last.'

'What?'

'I'm not sure. Seems to be many isolated things. But something big is happening. It can be felt in the underworld.'

'What is it?'

'I'll tell you on the way.'

'Where are we going?'

'I think they've found the prison.'

'What prison?'

'The prison where the boy-warrior is kept.'

4

They made their way like fugitives through a night of jackals. It was pitch black in spite of the sweating moon. They wandered through desolated tenements, giant council estates with gut-rot on the walls, through wastelands where the arm or leg of some victim of the night rotted among the accumulated junk of the streets.

They made their cautious way through a night of howls and cries that pierced the silence. The howls came from darkened houses, from grim sleepers.

The bookshop girl wore her jackal mask. Sometimes Karnak was not sure whether she had changed or not. Once turning a corner, the mask brushed his shoulder and he shouted involuntarily.

'What's wrong with you?' she said.

'I think I saw them devour a man tonight. I still haven't recovered from the shock of it. Do you have to wear that thing?'

'I feel safer with it. Among jackals you must seem a jackal. How safe do you feel with your normal face?'

At that moment they heard grunting noises coming towards them. The sounds were punctuated with rough laughter, and then a howl of raw pleasure. Then more grunting. They hid behind a garden wall and watched as three men, jackal-faced, dragged behind them the corpse of a woman.

They waited a long time before they emerged from their hiding place. When the grunting and rough laughter receded, they broke into a run. Ruslana put her mask back on. It was clear that nowhere was safe.

They heard broken howls coming from the distant houses. Sometimes it sounded as if a whole household was being butchered. They kept close to the hedges, crouching as they ran to avoid being seen. Thick clouds darkened the sky and across the land a ghostly sigh could be heard, as though the wind were drawing its last breath in the evil hour.

They made their way through the streets, taking short cuts through the gaps between buildings. They came to a woodland that led up a hill. Ruslana seemed more at ease. She took off the mask and stopped walking.

'Bodies are being washed up on the shores of the river. Parts of bodies are being found in cellars, or on rubbish dumps. People are returning from the grave.'

She paused, then said:

'But when the bodies were inspected they were found to have come from the other side of the world. They are not our bodies.'

She paused again.

'Have you heard the rumours?'

'Which ones? I've heard so many.'

'The latest ones.'

'No.'

She took a deep breath and began to climb the hill. It was

the hill where the boy-warrior was first sighted in the attire of a fool. The wind rushed up the steep hill and they found it hard climbing in the dark. Clouds massed in the sky. Howls and cries from all over the city seemed to converge on these heights.

'They are going to torture and kill him, unless something happens,' she said suddenly, in the dark. 'If they kill him, they kill something in all of us.'

5

The hill they climbed was more like a mountain. They were climbing for a long time and still they were on the lower slopes. The earth was soft as if it had rained. But it hadn't rained. The plants were hardier and sparser as they ascended. Trees gave way to shrubs, shrubs gave way to gorse. The earth was drier. The screen of furze all around made it hard to see.

They went in silence along a trail that unfolded in the dark. There were times when the trail was invisible and when they weren't sure they were on the right path. But Karnak followed Ruslana unquestioningly. She moved with sureness in the dark, as if her feet could see. She walked without doubt and she rose steadily.

Sometimes the path became visible. When it was visible it gave off a yellow light but Karnak was sure he was imagining this. They clambered up in silence, but there were wafts of fading screams, falling howls, rising cries, from the distant sleepers.

As they rose Karnak saw a yellow-green star pulsing in the depths of the sky. He watched it as he ascended. The earth became stonier. They may have been scaling the rough paths of a mountain. They climbed silently for a while. Then Ruslana stopped. She was no longer holding her mask.

She had stopped because she was looking up at something

Karnak had not seen. When he looked up his heart heaved in wonder that he had been chosen to see this sight. He felt himself unworthy. He knew at once that he was seeing something rare, a vision in real life.

He felt like those seekers of old who beheld, in the golden breath of a moment, the mysterious image of initiation. He felt like those secret alchemists who, after a lifetime of experimentation and dedication, finally witness the transformation of an ingot of lead into the immortal lustre of gold.

High on the highest crag of the mountain he saw the figure of an ancient hermit, clad in the grey mantle of night. On his head was a blue cap shaped like the tenth letter of the Hebrew alphabet. The lantern he held aloft shone as a six-pointed star. The light from the lantern streamed downwards, intermittently illuminating the path.

6

They resumed their climb. Sometimes they saw the light from the lamp and sometimes they didn't. They rose steadily till they reached an eminence. They could see clearly all around. The gorse had fallen away to reveal many thousands of people, all with little lamps, making their way up the sides of the mountain. They formed a moving constellation of lights on the dark earth.

'Who are all these people?' Karnak asked.

'I don't know,' Ruslana said. 'But they're a sign.'

'Of what?'

'That something is happening.'

They went on with their path. As they climbed, so did the others. They moved with the massed forces of their lights, pursuing their steady ascent till they were as high as they could get, given the nature of the paths. The people with their lights formed a strange congregation, all around the high peak, in the dark. The stars in the sky had nestled down on the mountainside. The people waited and were still.

High above them, on what must have been an ancient crag from the lost ages of the mountain, the hermit stood, holding his lamp aloft. But for the curious illumination of his lantern he could have been a figure carved from the rock of night. It seemed as if he were perched on a rock and at the same time standing on a cloud. He was silent. All they could hear was the wind in the sky and the howling in the city. Then not even the howls were heard as they listened to the hermit's silence.

There are many conflicting views of what happened next. But the result was the same. Some said that in the silence the hermit made a speech which was carried around by a swirling wind. Some said the hermit said nothing, but in the nothing they saw and heard things. Some saw the image of an emperor sitting on a cubic stone. A ram's head projected out of the side of the stone. Some saw the image of a prison. It was part of the night. It was square and mighty and dark. Some saw the image of a tower struck by lightning. Some said they heard a new sermon on the mount.

The real effect of whatever they had seen or heard was that the hermit disappeared. It happened at an unknown moment in the night when there was a shift in the constellation. Thrown back on themselves when the dazzling light from the hermit's lamp was no longer there, the multitude at last acted. They poured back down the mountainside. They moved in mantled silence, holding their individual lights aloft, an army of lights descending the mountain. As they went down, a voice, the voice of the bookshop girl, cried:

'To the tower! Let's destroy the tower!'

7

No one had ever seen the Hierarchy. No one knew what the Hierarchy looked like. The people had been governed by them for generations, but they had never seen those who governed them.

They had never seen the tower either. Its existence had been a persistent rumour from the underworld which had acquired the reality of fact. But no one had ever seen it. There had never been any references to it in public communications or official circulars or edicts. The Hierarchy had no head-quarters known to the people. As far as the people knew, the Hierarchy did not need headquarters. In the popular mind the Hierarchy was not a people. It did not have members. It did not meet in any place. The Hierarchy simply was. It existed. It was numinous. Its powers extended beyond time and space.

To the people, the Hierarchy had control over the weather, over night and day, over the flow of rivers, over the growth of crops. The Hierarchy was the power that governed, dictated, enforced. It was the invisible will. It was the central power without a name, without faces. It had power over destiny.

The Hierarchy was omnipotent. It dwelt with every man and woman and child. It was everyone's dreams. It was good and evil. It was past and present and future. The Hierarchy was everywhere.

It was beyond thought that the Hierarchy would meet in a

place, or that it had anything resembling a physical organisation. No one had ever thought such a thought. The populace lived with its notion of the Hierarchy under the darkness of a mountain, under the wings of a giant bird bigger than the sky.

But with rumours and signs pouring out of the underworld, this notion was beginning to crack.

That night as they poured down the mountainside, as they poured towards the tower that they had never seen and did not know existed, they were changing the world as they knew it.

8

Ruslana led the multitudes the same way she had climbed the mountain in the dark; she seemed to follow a road that only she could see. Someone had given her a lamp and it shone like a six-pointed star. Behind her, the multitudes, like a silent army, streamed down the mountainside. Their only weapons were their little lamps. They were a slowly flowing river, heavy with all its silted weight.

Karnak stayed close by the side of Ruslana and the strange lamp. He marvelled at how she had changed in such a short time. She had become a force of destiny, leading the swelling multitudes down the hill and into the quiet streets of the city. As they flowed down the streets, sleepers and howlers in their houses woke up, overcame their bewilderment and joined them. Houses woke and emptied as the multitudes with their lights flowed past.

In what seemed like no time the clamorous river of people occupied the streets. Their lights had multiplied and they brought some of the day into the night.

A banner had appeared in Ruslana's hand. It had one word on it in red capital letters, one word that had long perplexed the sleeping populace:

UPRISE!

Like a dark flood, the multitudes filled the streets. With its infinite points of light, a constellation visible in the city, they swarmed towards the famous square. The bookshop girl led them through the maze of the streets. They went round and round the city, took many turns, came up against dead ends, and turned back on themselves. They pressed on with undiminished spirit. The night had turned the city into a labyrinth.

Ruslana walked as if in a trance, with a strange smile on her face. Suddenly she stopped at a vast empty field. Slowly, in silence, the crowds surged towards her and stopped. They stared silently into the darkness of the field.

Then as they stared they saw that the field was not a field but a chasm, an abyss. As they went on staring they saw that it was not a chasm or an abyss. Under their concentrated gaze, it resolved itself into something no one had seen before. It had only been heard about in rumours sprung from the underground.

They saw before them the great dark tower forgotten in legend. It was thirteen storeys high and built on a massive base of rock. In silence and fear they gazed upon the dark tower. They saw that it had three windows, in the form of downward pointing triangles. They also saw that at the summit of the tower was a giant bronze crown.

With their little lights held aloft, the people crowded round the tower. Incomprehension flowed around them like the wind.

9

The authorities unleashed the fierce police on the crowd and the silence was broken. There was pandemonium everywhere as the jackal-headed police devoured the people; they shot them, clubbed them, and ate them. The police ripped off the arms and legs of the people, chewed off their heads, and ate their way through the multitudes.

Intoxicated by their rage for order, they ate their way through the crowds. They ate the lanterns and the little lights too.

They must have devoured hundreds of people and as many lamps when something peculiar happened. No one knows how it happened and it has never been explained. A collective sigh rose from the multitudes. Then a silence settled on everyone. For an eternal moment in the pandemonium there was a strange glacial silence. For a moment a curious stillness reigned. It may have been because of the sound of a sublime trumpet.

There was something soul-piercing about it. No one had ever heard such a tone before. It was beyond all the registers of sound. It played above their heads as though an angel of the apocalypse were blasting forth the celestial trumpet for the waking of the dead from their graves.

The sound was brief and piercing and women threw their hands up in exultation and men crossed their arms in front of their chests in a hieratic sign of supplication. Some claimed afterwards that the sound came from the underworld. Some said that it was a rare moment of the interpenetration of a higher world with this one. Those who did not believe in such inexplicable things maintained that it was the natural conclusion of a historic progression, when the forces deep in the human spirit revolt against its oppression, and that the sound heard was the collective cry of a rebellion so momentous that it altered the powers in the world. Whatever the sound was, from whatever realm it came, whether from within the multitudes, or from elsewhere, it had shattering consequences. There are moments in history that cannot be explained by the normal modes of explanation. They are causes of wonder and border on the miraculous. They are frightening to historians. They are the territory of myth.

When this inexplicable sound blasted over the pandemonium the fierce police with their jackal-faces stood transfixed. Their mouths were red with the blood of the living men and women they had devoured. But the immeasurable sound made them stand still, as if they had been turned to stone.

When the sound passed, people in the crowds woke from the dream it had induced, and everyone stood around a little stunned to find themselves where they were. Many were surprised to find themselves in the streets in their pyjamas. Many were astonished to find themselves awake. But maybe the most astonished of all were the fierce police of the Hierarchy. They found that they had lost their jackal-faces.

They stood among the crowd with their half-confused normal faces, with the blood and an unnatural bitter taste in their mouths.

Almost in an instant, as if an inaudible command had been uttered, the police beat a retreat and sped away in their white vans and armoured vehicles.

10

Released from the enchantment of ages, the crowd clamoured round the foot of the rock. They clambered up the base of the tower, till they formed an intense gathering. Then with shouts and songs, with prayers and curses, they shook the tower. They heaved and rocked the structure.

They must have shifted something significant for a great cry was heard from the heights of the tower. Then a bolt of lightning, which seemed to come from a momentarily visible solar disc, struck the bronze crown at the summit. Then the bronze crown, made by artisans of old, came tumbling down. It fell with a resounding crash into the abyss on the north side.

While the crowd recovered from the shock of the falling crown, they saw people jumping from the three windows. Fires had broken out all over the tower. Fires blazed from the three windows, forming dense clouds in seven places round about the tower.

Those who jumped from the tower were seen falling upside down, screaming as they fell. Some fell into the abyss. Those who jumped from the burning windows smashed on to the ground.

11

The crowds gathered to see who the Hierarchy were. They gathered to see what they were. They gathered round in curiosity. Murmurs and rumours circulated among them. They clustered round the fallen broken bodies. They were surprised to see that the bodies were broken and smashed and bleeding. With trepidation, with fear, they turned the bodies over, expecting perhaps to see something unimaginable. To their horror they saw that the bodies were the bodies of people they knew and recognised. They saw themselves. They saw that the Hierarchy members were people just like them. They saw that the Hierarchy was them and that they were the Hierarchy. They and the Hierarchy were one. They had always been one.

12

Confused by this revelation that they had inflicted oppression and terror on themselves for centuries, the people hung their heads in silence and shame and distress.

The people who had smashed to the ground were little people like them. Their blood oozed out of broken skulls. Their arms and legs, all broken, were like the arms and legs of the dead and dying. They were no different from all those who had been devoured by the jackal-faces, no different from all those who howled at night as though all hope had fled the earth.

The crowd would have collapsed beneath the weight of its own incomprehension were it not for the spirit and exhortations of Ruslana. Waving her banner, shouting the one word into the centre of their gloom, rousing their courage, the bookshop girl led them towards the mythical prison built in the dead centre of the land.

13

The prison was the single greatest structure in the world and it cast an enormous shadow. It was made of lead, concrete, iron, adamant, volcanic rock, stout steel, and organic substances of unusually tough material. It was the forbidding masterwork of the Hierarchy.

It was the work of innumerable generations. It was believed to have been built at the beginning of time and it was referred to in this way in the new myths. Successive eras of evolution, technology, philosophy, and intentionality had gone into its aggregate construction. Its foundation went deep into the earth. It was like a gigantic mausoleum.

The prison had three levels. Outwardly it was shaped like a pyramid but with five sides instead of four. Each side, made of the toughest metals, had a single window. The window was always darkened.

It was a compact mass of darkness and force, so tall it blotted out the sky. The whole area around it was a dead zone.

The prison was the heart of the land, its greatest symbol. It was the land. Though no one had ever seen the prison before, because of the force-field around it that had rendered it invisible, all roads and all destinies led to the prison.

14

The prison was the mind and heart of the land. To glimpse it was to sense things previously unknown about it. You would sense its innumerable vaulted ceilings, its black and white pillars of ancient construction, diverse materials, and noble forms. You would sense its massive staircases that led to nightmare interiors which bristled with the limitless memory of the land. You would sense its massive gates, wrought with figures of death, a large skeleton with a scythe, possessing a huge skull from which two serpents crawled out of its eye-sockets, and the crossed bones in bronze high above the gates.

To glimpse the prison was to see that it was the home of the original labyrinth. All those who entered were lost forever in its holes, its winding spaces, its limitless cellars, its oblique torture chambers, its vast hall of mirrors, its tunnels, its passageways that led to obscure depths. Its dungeons were magnificent and housed many wondrous and fearful things.

It was a house of noise and silence. It had monstrous rooms of seven walls. It had vaults of the forgotten dead. It was the centre of the land.

15

When the people dreamt it was to the prison that they went. The prison was the temple of the land. The Hierarchy had made it the centre of the land's new religion. From the prison were conducted all the rigorous obscure rites. Here priests were ordained. From here the economy was run. The prison was the true centre of government.

There was a numinous relationship between the Hierarchy and the prison. But the relationship between the prison and all aspects of the land was unknown, till it was glimpsed for the first time.

16

They had poured towards the prison, they had crowded towards it in rage. They had wanted to destroy it, to tear it down. But as they gazed upon its monumental structure they were struck dumb. It was the wonder of the ages, the single greatest achievement of the race.

They found themselves gazing at that which had been built by their desires, their fears, their hopes, their blood, their dreams. Their ancestors had built it brick by brick, stone upon stone, metal upon metal, not knowing what it was they were building. They had built it and consecrated it with their daily lives. They thought they were building the noblest work known to man and woman, for the glorification of the ages.

Many millions had perished in its construction. The sea, the earth, the air, and the remote stars had collaborated in the erection of this monstrous structure that stood like a mountain on the flat earth.

While they gazed upon it the multitudes realised they were gazing upon something else, something that made them silent. They gazed almost without breathing. Each person became aware that they carried around within them the prison they gazed upon. Each person was aware of being in prison themselves. Each person sensed now the forgotten passages from the original myth, which said that, after the fall, in the beginning was the prison.

17

Hanging upside down, in the depths of the prison, in its deepest dungeon, the boy-warrior remembered his grandfather reading to him from the book of the original myth. He remembered what the old man had said before he died.

'One day, my boy, you must take a leap into the unknown and discover what has been hidden from us. Don't be like the rest of us. Follow your best nature. Follow your deepest questions. The world is the wrong way up. Up is down and down is up. Things are not what they seem. Follow the trails left in the original myths. Everything we need to know is concealed in what we take for granted. There are many prisons within prisons. There are many prisons outside prisons too. But there is a boundless horizon. It is not out there. It is not above or below. It is not out there in space or at the bottom of the sea. It is the only freedom there is from all the prisons. No one has found it for a thousand years. Find it and bring the discovery back to your people that they may each start on the journey to the ultimate freedom.'

18

The boy hanging upside down knew that no one had ever escaped the prison. He knew from fragments of the original myth that no one had ever escaped the prison because the prison was not a building. It was not a structure or a form. No one had ever escaped the prison because the prison was the world. It was the world of the living and the dead. These were things he had glimpsed from the original myths.

It was maybe at that moment that the boy-warrior had the great revelation that had been growing in him all the days of his life. For he suddenly saw a roseate fire all around him. He saw the roseate fire and he beheld a great light shining through the prison. It shone through the walls and bars, through its lead and its stone. It shone through its crypts and torture chambers and labyrinths as though all that stone and iron were as insubstantial as air.

19

The silent multitudes saw a strange light shining in the prison and they were afraid. In the depths of the night the prison seemed transfigured. For a fugitive moment it seemed to be covered in splendour. It was radiant with a golden glow, as if the prison itself housed the rising sun.

A deep collective howl was heard. It came from all over the land, from the earth itself. Like a flight of demons, the howls escaped into the air, into what was left of the night. Then the howls faded into the corners of the sky.

It is recorded that the waters tasted sweet that night. Changes were noted in the depths of rivers.

20

With the first star of dawn, an amazing thing came to pass. With no turning of the keys in the locks, the gates of the prison opened and the doors were unbolted. The boy, no longer the boy-warrior, was seen coming out of the prison. He looked tiny beneath those gigantic gates. The massive skeleton with the scythe suddenly looked harmless.

They had expected a hero, but they saw a child. They saw a child who had once been read to by an old man. A child who had been read to from the original myth.

He came out of the prison with a playful smile on his face. He smiled as though the world was a child's game played in eternity.

As the multitudes beheld him they sensed the wheels of fortune change. The child seemed to them the very image of the world as it should be.

Once she took him to the top of a high hill in the centre of the city. It was early in the afternoon, on a weekend, and the view of the city was clear and fine. They sat on a bench and looked out over the splendid view of the city in silence. Then she began to sing. She sang quietly to herself. Then she stopped. Karnak looked at her when she stopped. He saw that she was weeping.

'What's wrong?'

'Nothing.'

'Then why are you weeping?'

'No reason really.'

'There must be. What is it?'

Amalantis didn't say anything for a while.

'This world could be so beautiful,' she said.

Not long after that they came for her.

21

Out of the prison, behind the boy, came a great procession of those who had disappeared into the endless dark. Like the creatures saved on a fabled ark, they poured forth from the immense prison. They poured out onto the tempered earth. They came out of the prison like ghosts. There were so many. No one knew that so many had been lost in the dark. They poured out like shadows and when they came out into the air they acquired substance again. They were coming out of the night and into the dawn.

Among them were the artists and the writers and the scientists and inventors and the politicians who had told awkward truths. Among them were children and lost mothers and Ruslana's father and other fathers.

There was among them a woman who seemed to be dancing, holding a magic wand in each hand. And there was one who carried what looked like a celestial wheel.

Not inconspicuously among them was also the hierophant and his two acolytes. Each of the acolytes bore a book containing fragments of the original myth. The books brought back into the world the mystery of the lost word.

22

Karnak studied each face in the procession. He looked at each face with a shaking heart. He saw how each new face was greeted with cries of intemperate joy from someone in the crowd. He saw Ruslana weep with jubilation at being reunited with her father. He came out of the prison and paused beneath its gate with a tranquil expression on his face. He was gaunt but lit with a magical light.

One after another those returning from the dark were received with shouts of inhuman happiness or with the silence of an unimaginable reunion. And the young lover waited and watched each face with a heart heaving and a heart trembling with hope.

He looked at each face knowing that one of them could be the love of his life that he had lost on a day when he was deep in the sleep of life.

And then he saw her. She was suddenly there beneath the gate. She was thin and serene and beautiful. There was something immeasurably different about her. He hurried towards her. She was gazing round at the world with calm, neutral eyes. When he got to where she stood, Karnak fell at her feet. Amalantis regarded him calmly, with a half-smile. Then she made him rise.

Coda

In the oldest legends of the land, it is known that all are born in prison.

In the new reality, all are born into a story. It is a story which everyone creates and which everyone lives, with darkness or with light, in freedom.

Little Venice
London